The Re-Appearing Statue

A Jackpine Point Adventure

The Re-Appearing Statue

Sandy Larsen

Merritt Park Press
Duluth, Minnesota

For Dr. Mac

Cover Art and Illustration by Wanda Taylor

ISBN 0-9666677-0-0
Library of Congress Catalog Card Number: 98-96504

6/00   P5T8

Fiction/Ages 10-14

Z 701834

Merritt Park Press
3912 W. 7th Street
Duluth MN 55807
dslarsen@spacestar.net
(218) 628-0618

Table of Contents

I'm David Malloy,
and my friends and I live out on Jackpine Point.

That's where a lot of jackpines grow.
They're not a great-looking tree. But they're tough.

Jackpines grow places where other trees can't.
They're the first trees to spring up after a forest fire
because the heat of the fire pops open the cones
and lets the seeds out.

Some people say jackpines
have to go through fire
if they're going to grow at all.

1

I Spend A Lot of Time in Ditches

The best place to start telling you this story is when I jumped off my bike as it flew down a steep bank into a ditch full of water. I heard two giant splashes. One was my bike and the other was me.

Then came another, *bigger* giant splash. Marmy Albright and her bike had hit the cold weedy ditch together.

Not a good way to start the first Saturday in October.

So there I was again, in an uncomfortable mess, all because Dillon and Marmy wanted me to help them get Ripper Wilter. In case you don't know who Ripper is—and then I'll explain why I was in the ditch—he moved here to Bell Harbor last year from the big city. Everybody said he was really mean. I kept out of his way till the day I accidentally crashed into him in the cafeteria and spilled Tuna Surprise all over his front and shoes. That's when he leaned into my face and growled, "I'll get you, David Malloy! I eat people like you for lunch and nails for dessert!"

You see? I guess everybody has to have a Ripper in their lives, but why do *I* have to have one? That's what I keep asking Miss Wainwright.

And you know what she keeps telling me? "If your enemy is hungry, feed him."

That sounded okay in our classroom at church. Now, hiding in that cold ditch with my head barely out of the water, it sounded like advice from Neptune.

I mean, how could throwing Ripper a sandwich get me out of this?

Ripper's tires whizzed past on the road above, and I ducked. I didn't care if he was hungry. I just wanted to know, was he *stopping?* I sucked in a big breath and held it. I think my face was getting blue but of course I couldn't see if it was or not.

He was going on past. The buzz of the tires got smaller and farther away.

I breathed again, waited until I felt slightly less scared, and stood up among the weeds. Muddy water poured off me. A big wet cattail was hanging across my head. I spit out feathery seeds and looked around.

Nobody in sight.

"Marmy?"

No answer.

I hoped she hadn't drowned or something worse. I risked

10

calling a little louder. "Marmy? Hey, where are you?"

A voice screeched close behind my right ear: "Quiet!! You want Ripper to catch us?!"

I picked myself up out of the water where I'd fallen on my face from shock. Then I turned around. Slowly— because of my great self-control and also because I was freezing. Last night's chill was still in that ditch water.

"Marmalade," I said through my shivering teeth, "if you ever do that again . . ."

What I'd do I never found out, because directly between us Dillon McBride stood up through the cattails with water running off him from everywhere and hollered, "Will *both* of you shut up before Ripper comes back and finds us!"

Dillon had been riding ahead and hit the ditch before Marmy and me. He gets me into all kinds of stuff and he's not very good at getting me out, but he can holler like anything.

I tried pulling my bike out of the water. It was tangled in weeds. Frogs plopped around me, probably laughing their little green legs off at how silly I looked.

I yanked the cattail off my face and discovered I could see better. Dillon was twisting the water out of the tail of his T-shirt. Marmy was doing the same thing with her hair.

"We've got to get back and warn the other Pointers," Dillon said, wiping his wet hands on his even wetter jeans.

Marmy made an ugly face at an even uglier beetle she'd found in her hairdo. "Yeah," she said, "we've got to tell them Ripper Wilter just tried to make us into sausage. If he's after us, he's after all the Pointers."

That was true. See, my friends and I go to school in Bell Harbor, but we all live out on Jackpine Point. We ride the bus together and do practically everything together.

11

The Point is a great place to live. It's rocky and woodsy, and there's one road that runs the length of it—the Point road, of course—with the bay on one side and the Big Lake on the other. None of us would want to live anywhere else in Bell Harbor or for that matter anywhere else on earth.

But you need to understand, all kinds of things happen to us Pointers that don't happen to ordinary people.

I mean, we *are* ordinary people, sort of, but we're also champions at having adventures that don't start out that way and that we don't mean to be adventures. I guess Miss Wainwright said it best. "Wherever the Jackpine Pointers are," she said, "you know something is going to *occur.*"

Well, things had been *occurring* left and right since the day Ripper Wilter came to town.

Where was I? Oh, yeah, still in the ditch. So anyway the three of us helped each other get our bikes out of the water. Pulling cattails out of his chain, Dillon said, "David, go up the bank and scout to see if everything is all clear."

I had a better idea. "Why don't *you* go scout and see if everything is all clear?"

"I have to get the cattails out of my chain."

"Well, I have to get the cattails out of my ears." I looked at Marmy for help, but she was busy dumping water out of her shoes. I sighed and pushed my bike up the bank.

The sun was warm and welcoming on the blacktop road. Nobody else was in sight.

"Come on," I called down to the others. "We'll stop at Brownie's orchard on the way home."

We rode along slowly, keeping a lookout and letting the sun warm us up. Dillon said I had to go first, but then he pedaled up beside me and asked a question that about knocked me off my bike. He asked, "Why do you suppose Ripper's after us?"

"Have you lost your memory?" I squawked. "Don't you remember last night we sneaked up the alley behind his house, got into his garage, tripped over a lawn mower, knocked his bike into a garbage bag full of pop cans, and made so much noise that the lights went on and every dog in town started barking and we got out of there just in time to save ourselves from . . . ." I was running out of breath, getting more and more worked up thinking about that awful night last night.

"He's got no right to get mad at *us*," Marmy said as she pedaled alongside. "We were just trying to get Dillon's roller blades back because Ripper stole them."

"Yeah," Dillon added. "It's not our fault his garage has one of those old wood doors that doesn't shut all the way. It's not like we were breaking and entering. We just . . . . slipped in."

Marmy wasn't finished. She never is. "Anyhow, how does he know it was us? Lots of people are mad at Ripper Wilter. He's stolen a lot of people's stuff. I heard in the city he was in some kind of gang, and they went around swiping anything they felt like."

"Maybe," I said, "just maybe he guessed who it was because he heard both of you screaming at the top of your lungs as you ran off down the alley."

Dillon changed the subject like he always does. "Here's Brownie's orchard. We'd better tell him to be on the lookout for Ripper."

We turned our bikes into the lane that leads through Brownie's orchard to his trailer.

I should explain, it isn't really Brownie's own personal orchard. His parents work there taking care of it, so he gets to live there. It's an apple orchard. His family, the Browns— his real name's Bobby Brown—his family doesn't have much money, so we're all supposed to feel sorry for him and give him our old clothes and stuff. Actually we all think he's kind of lucky. He's got miles of apple trees to run around in, and a Labrador retriever, and he wears shirts with holes in them, but if I get a hole in one of my shirts I have to throw it away.

I was thinking how unfair it is that life is unfair when I saw Brownie running down the lane toward us, waving both arms. "Wow, is he glad to see us!" Marmy said, waving back. Brownie waved even harder. Dillon and I waved too, and Brownie waved even more.

My arms were getting tired when he got close enough to talk to us. In the world's loudest whisper he ordered, "Stop waving! Ripper Wilter's up at my house looking for you! He's checking out my tree house this minute because he thinks you're hiding there."

I didn't like how Brownie looked at *me* when he said *"you."* "You mean he thinks all of us are hiding there?"

"I mean *you,* David Malloy! He says last night you stole something out of his garage."

"Me! What does he think I stole?"

"His Little League batting trophy. He says it's his most prized possession. He also says you knocked over two thousand pop cans and made so much noise he knew it was a real amateur, because nobody in the city would do things that way. Anyway he heard you screaming at the top of

14

your lungs as you ran off down the alley. Look, in two seconds he'll be down from that tree, so get going!"

I started to protest that I hadn't stolen anything, but Brownie pushed me toward the ditch at the edge of the lane. "He's coming! And he's mad!"

No. Not another ditch. I was trying to explain how I'd promised myself I'd never hide in another wet ditch when Brownie put both hands on top of my head and shoved me down. The last thing I heard him say was "Malloy, why are you so wet? You look like you just got out of a ditch." Then I heard ferocious barking and bike tires on gravel and somebody yelling "Call her off! Call her off! You'll be sorry for this, Brownie!" and what sounded like a Fourth of July parade shot past me going out toward the road and then it was gone.

I waited a few seconds and stuck my head up. Brownie was standing there grinning, looking in the direction where the noise had gone. Then he whistled and clapped, and his black Lab, Sugar, galloped up holding a Twins cap in her teeth. It looked a lot like the one Ripper Wilter wears 25 hours a day. Well, he wasn't wearing it now.

Sugar dropped the cap at Brownie's feet and sat smiling and panting and drooling and thumping her tail on the ground.

Marmy screeched, "David, it's all over for you! That's Ripper's Twins cap! He wears it all the time! Look what that dog did to it! You're in for it now!" I think she would have gone on all day.

"Who cares?" I said. "I'm going home." Just between us, I sounded braver than I felt. "Ripper can't think much of his Little League trophy if he keeps it out in that leaky garage. Anyway he was so scared by that dog he's probably

15

home hiding under his bed right now." I hoped that was true, but I can't say I totally believed it.

I patted Sugar on the head, wrung out Ripper's Twins cap, put it on, took it off, and tossed it to Dillon, who jumped back like I'd tossed him a lit bottle rocket.

Brownie picked up the cap. "I'll wash it and give it to Ripper next week," he said, and I should have known something would go wrong with that, but I was too cold and tired. Dillon and Marmy and I went back out to the road and started coasting down the long hill toward home.

I felt better heading home from Brownie's orchard. I'm crazy about that part of the road. You come over the top of the hill and it's the most awesome sight in the world. There's the end of Jackpine Point below you and the Big Lake to your right, deep blue or reddish-brown or foggy or stirred up with whitecaps, and in winter there's ice stretching out from shore, sometimes farther than you can see. To your left the shore curves around into the bay, and that's where the town of Bell Harbor is.

This October morning the lake was shining blue. The woods glowed gold and orange, mixed with deep green spruce and pine for accents. Facing the bay, the town of Bell Harbor looked peaceful and friendly in the sunshine. You see all that and you thank God you live up here, even if "here" includes enemies like Ripper Wilter and friends whose great ideas get me into all kinds of tight spots because I'm a nice guy and I'm loyal to the Pointers. I was getting mad all over again.

Sorry, it just gets to me sometimes.

At the bottom of the hill we saw the fifth Jackpine Pointer coming toward us. It was Cathy Knutson out for her daily thinking walk.

I believe Cathy invented virtual reality. Anyway she sure lives there. She looks at you like you're one of those shapes on the computer screen made out of lines and she's trying to figure out how to rotate you in space. She takes walks by herself to think about big ideas that the rest of us don't understand.

We all said "Hey Cath!"

She looked at my face without exactly looking at me. In her head I could tell she was rolling that mouse around, walking inside those squares and circles.

"Cathy!" I said, "Listen! Ripper Wilter is after the Pointers. He stole Dillon's roller blades. He thinks we stole some dumb batting trophy of his. But we didn't steal anything. We've also got his Twins cap. I mean Brownie's dog has it. It's probably in the washing machine now. So watch out for yourself, okay?"

"Let's have a meeting Monday after school to figure out what to do." That was Marmy's suggestion.

"Let's ask Miss Wainwright what to do Sunday." That was Dillon's suggestion.

"Let's interface with Cath's operating system so she can read us." That was my suggestion.

I jumped when I heard Cathy's voice. I wasn't sure she was even occupying the same planet with us. "Oh, I get it," she said. "You think Ripper's a thief and he thinks we're thieves. But he is and we're not. So he's out to smash us."

I'd gotten through after all. You never know with her.

"Okay then," I told everybody, "watch out for yourselves

and we'll meet at my house on . . ." I never was good at keeping a calendar in my head. "What day is this anyway?"

Cath punched a button on her watch. "It's Saturday, October the wunth."

I blinked and said "Saturday October the what?"

"Saturday, October the wunth."

I thought about that. "Don't you mean the first?"

"Oh, yeah, thanks. Saturday, October the first."

That's Cath for you. When she can't remember a word, she makes up a new one, and the one she makes up is so much better than the one she forgot that you wonder why they didn't put it in the dictionary in the first place.

I got curious about something. "What's tomorrow?"

She punched the button on her watch again and said "I don't know, it doesn't say yet."

That was disappointing. I wanted to hear her say "Sunday, October the tooth."

Actually it was Monday, October the threeth when all five of us Pointers got together again at my house after school.

Marmy and Dillon and I had told Miss Wainwright a little about the situation on Sunday when we went to her class. Brownie and Cathy don't go to church, except now and then the rest of us have dragged them to a special youth event or something.

When we told Miss Wainwright about Ripper and his trophy, all she said was "Tell the truth and trust the Lord to take care of the rest. And don't forget, if your enemy is hungry, feed him."

I wondered what kind of candy Ripper liked. Probably Rusty Nail Bars.

The other Pointers had arrived at my house and we were in the basement rec room digging into some of my Mom's chocolate chip cookies, when my Dad came downstairs.

"David," he said, "I need to ask you and your friends about something."

"Can it wait a minute, Dad?" I said, stuffing my mouth with cookies with my back to him. "We're having a mrdg."

"You're having a what?"

"A mrdg," I said, spitting crumbs.

"He means a meeting, Mr. Malloy," Dillon explained. "He's got his mouth full as usual."

But Dads aren't discouraged easily. "Isn't there somebody in your class named Richard Wilter?"

Marmy spoke up, "You bet there is! That's Ripper." She had a mouthful of cookies too, but nothing stops her from talking. "You've heard us talk about Ripper. He was new last year. From the city. He was in a gang or something and he hates the Pointers and he'd like to turn us into sausage."

I heard Dad say, "Well then don't you think it's funny that I found this in our garage?"

I couldn't see what he meant by "this." But I felt cold all the way through, like I'd taken another dive into freezing water. I turned slowly around like I was back in that ditch.

In my Dad's hands I saw a shiny, silvery object. It was shaped amazingly like a person with a baseball bat about to hit a homer.

In big letters on the wooden base it said:

Little League

And in even bigger letters it said:

CHAMPION
RICHARD WILTER

2

I Get Caught in a Dark Alley

I couldn't figure out how Ripper had won *two* trophies. Side by side and both of them exactly alike. Then my eyes cleared up and I saw there was only one trophy, which was still one more than I wanted to see.

I opened my mouth to explain how this statue thing had gotten into our garage. But since I had no idea, all I could do was squeak.

Then I heard Cathy Knutson say, "Somebody must have put it there."

That sounded really smart. I agreed with her. "Yeah!

Somebody must have put it there!" It didn't sound nearly as smart when I said it as when Cath did. Nothing ever does.

Dad announced in that heavy voice he uses for special occasions such as this, "Well, I hope one of you didn't swipe it and hide it there as a joke."

The silver statue came floating through the air straight at me. I retreated backwards and stabbed myself in the back with the corner of the ping-pong table. Dillon was saying, "Take it, David, he's trying to give it to you!"

"I don't want it!" I howled—but the thing was in my hands. Now I felt really guilty. I heard my Dad's voice going back up the stairs: "Well no matter how it got there, you'll have to take it back to Ripper—I mean Richard."

Funny. Three trophies now. Or was it four? I set all of them down on the ping-pong table on the far side of the net, crammed a cookie in my mouth, and looked around at the other Pointers.

You know how it is when an army is outnumbered 40,000 to 1 and they've run out of ammunition and the Weather Channel says it's about to snow three feet deep right on top of their tents? Well, that's how the Jackpine Pointers looked now, only worse.

It was definitely what Miss Wainwright would call a David-versus-Goliath situation.

Brownie opened his mouth first: "Let's everybody stay calm."

I glared at him and was about to say something brilliant and biting, except I couldn't think of anything, when my memory flashed. "His Twins cap!" I yelled. "You've got Ripper's Twins cap!"

"Let's everybody stay *real* calm," Brownie said.

"No, listen! You've still got his hat, right? You've got to

take it back to him, right? So give him his trophy at the same time. Tell him Sugar had it. Have her put a few teeth marks in it so it looks convincing. No, on second thought don't. But just give it back to him and then we'll . . ."

Brownie's face told me clearly that he was not going to volunteer for this mission.

Dillon announced, "There's only one thing to do."

Already I felt my teeth grinding against each other. Any idea of Dillon's about what to do meant one thing: *I* would have to do it. And it wouldn't be fun.

I waved him off. "Don't say it! You're going to say we have to take this thing back to Ripper. You're going to say we can't just hand it to him because then he'll think we took it. You're going to say the only thing to do is go to his house tonight and sneak it back into his garage from where we took it from—from whence we from took it—from whuther we—"

Marmalade shrieked, "Dillon, that's a great idea! You're a genius!"

"Thanks," Dillon said humbly.

"But we can't all go stomping into his garage together," Cathy pointed out. "One of us will have to do it alone."

"That's right," Brownie agreed. "It'll have to be the quietest one of us."

"That's not me!" Cathy said very loudly. Louder, in fact, than I'd ever heard her say anything.

"Me neither!" That booming voice was Brownie.

"Well *I* can't do it!" I was impressed. I had no idea Dillon could talk so loud.

I heard Marmalade suck in a big breath, but I motioned her to be quiet. After all these years I didn't need to hear her prove how loud she could be.

Well, if they thought they were the superstars of loudness, they hadn't heard from David Malloy. I paused to go over my turndown speech: thank you very much for this opportunity, but I regret I am unable to accept this honor.

I took a giant breath and launched my speech. All that came out was a squeak. Not a very loud one, either.

"See!" Marmy said. "You're perfect for the job!" I think everybody applauded. In despair I went to eat another cookie, but they were all gone.

A few hours later I could have used some applause in my ears. I was sneaking down the alley behind Ripper Wilter's house, clutching that silver you-know-what under my jacket.

If your enemy is hungry, feed him, huh? So what was I supposed to do, glue a chocolate-chip cookie to that batter's little metal head?

The other four Pointers were hiding in the bushes at the end of the alley. When it came down to it, they couldn't leave me to do this job all alone. We always stick together. Through thick and thin. Through wet and dry. Through cold and heat. Through wind and fire and earthquake and—

"Going somewhere, Malloy?"

That voice! Only centimeters behind me! Was it the Lord? No, it was the last person in the universe I wanted to meet in a dark alley.

I stayed calm, sort of. Without turning around I said, "Hi there, Ripper, how are you?" It wasn't very polite of me, but I couldn't stand seeing his face as well as hearing his voice. Meanwhile inside I started praying up a storm, a real gale-force northeaster like off the Big Lake.

"Okay," Ripper answered me.

Now there are lots of ways of saying "Okay," and this one was dangerous, if "Okay" can be dangerous, and believe me it can.

Feed your enemy. Feed your enemy. If I felt in my pockets, maybe I'd find a piece of gum or a linty gummy worm or something. Where were the other Pointers? Couldn't they see down the alley? Why weren't they coming to save me?

It seemed like it was my turn to say something, so I said, "Nice weather we're having."

I couldn't tell from Ripper's snort if he agreed with me about the weather, but it didn't matter because he changed the subject. "Need help with anything, Malloy?"

"Not really," I answered politely. I was on my way to becoming the prayer champ of Miss Wainwright's class plus listening for the rest of the Pointers all at the same time. "Thanks anyway."

"How about what you've got under your jacket?"

"Under my jacket? All I've got under my jacket is me."

Very slowly he replied "I . . . don't . . . think . . . so."

I started to state my innocence, but unfortunately right then I remembered I was guilty. If the others didn't show up in two seconds, I was doomed.

Well, for my own sake and the reputation of the Jackpine Pointers, I was going under bravely. I gathered up the micro sum of courage I still had and turned to face Ripper Wilter.

Ripper had changed. For one thing, he now looked exactly like Bobby Brown. His clothes looked like Brownie's. His hair looked like Brownie's. His face looked like Brownie's. As a matter of fact, he *was* Brownie.

"How do you like my Ripper imitation?" Brownie asked with disgusting pride.

"You nearly turned my hair white!" I hollered. "I never prayed so hard since last year when I took my math final!"

"Thanks. I've been practicing."

"Practicing! The only thing you'd better practice is taking stolen Little League batting trophies back to the people who own them!"

I whipped the silver statue out from under my jacket and shoved it into Brownie's hands. I thought he'd drop it like a chunk of hot lava. Instead, he took it and grinned.

"You know, when I was hiding back there, I was thinking," he said. "It's not really fair for you to have to do everything the rest of us think up, especially Dillon. Why should you do his dirty work? After all, it was *his* roller blades that Ripper stole."

I agreed completely with that idea. "Yeah. McBride ought to be doing this job and not me."

"Right. But do you think he'd do it?"

"Are you kidding? Dillon's all talk and no action. He gets me into all kinds of stuff."

"And never gets you out."

We stood there in the alley thinking dark thoughts about Dillon McBride. The problem was, this wasn't getting the trophy any closer to Ripper's garage. Then Brownie said something that about made my teeth fall out, if they hadn't been so firmly attached.

"I'll tell you what, David," he said, "I'll take the trophy back for you."

I stared at Brownie. He's been a good friend of mine for years, but I never thought he'd do something like this for me. Sure, I've given him some of my old sweatshirts, in fact he was wearing one of them now, the one that says BELL HARBOR ISN'T THE END OF THE WORLD, BUT IT'S RIGHT NEXT DOOR. Still I never thought he'd risk his neck for me like this.

"Brownie," I said, choking up a little, "you're just like it says, greater love nobody has than if somebody puts their life on the line for somebody."

"What are you talking about?"

"It's a quote."

"What from?"

"I can't remember. I'll ask Miss Wainwright."

"Do that. Well, I've got to get this crazy thing back to crazy Ripper's garage. Now get out of here before he sees you, okay?"

The next morning was the most bright and beautiful day that ever dawned on the face of the planet. Even if we had a pop quiz in every class, I knew I'd be ready. No matter how that trophy had gotten into my garage, it was safely returned to the owner. We'd escaped Ripper's fury. The five Jackpine Pointers were all talking and laughing at the same time when we got off the bus at school.

As the others went inside, I got inspired by an inspiration. I ran over to the corner store across the street. The owner was surprised when I went to pay for what I picked out.

"Getting a Baby Ruth today, David? You always get Snickers. I thought you didn't like Baby Ruths."

"I don't," I said. "It's not for me. It's for my enemy."

I ran back to the corner by the thorn hedge, where I knew Ripper Wilter would be coming in a little while. He walks just a few blocks to school, and he gets there at the last possible instant or afterward. I was so excited about what I was going to do that I almost forgot to be scared.

There he was! Zigzagging along the sidewalk, kicking stones left and right as he went. Probably practicing how to kick *me*. I waited, clutching the Baby Ruth in my fist. The wrapper was getting slippery with sweat. I wondered if fear could melt a chocolate coating.

Half a block away Ripper saw me and slowed up. His eyes squinted. I wondered if maybe he hadn't been out to his garage yet and didn't know the trophy was back. Should I yell and ask him? Should I try to explain? Should I run?

Ripper speeded up again and came toward me fast. I stood where I was. When he was one step away, I shoved the Baby Ruth straight at him.

He looked surprised. More than surprised. He looked from the candy bar to my face and back to the candy bar and to my face and so on. I didn't say anything. He didn't either.

Ripper Wilter grabbed the Baby Ruth out of my hand, unwrapped it, ate it, wadded up the wrapper, and ate the wrapper. Then he shoved me into the thorn hedge and spit the wrapper in my face.

"There's a catch to everything," I told Dillon when I got into school.

"What are you griping about?" he griped. He was trying to get the zipper on his backpack unstuck. "Brownie took the trophy back. Your problems are over. What about me?

28

Ripper's still got my roller blades. Say, why do you have prickly twigs in your hair?"

"You know that feed-your-enemy stuff Miss Wainwright talks about? Well, it doesn't work."

I told him what had happened. He stopped fooling with his backpack and looked like he was thinking hard, which I guess Dillon does every now and then.

"Well," he said at last, "it says to feed him, it doesn't say he'll thank you for it."

"Yeah. Like I said. There's a catch to everything."

As I got through the rest of that day, I felt better. At least I hadn't wasted a Snickers bar on Ripper.

After school the bus gets to Cathy Knutson's place first, so we did what we do a lot, we all got off there and played computer games and hung out and talked.

We'd been at Cathy's a half hour or so when somebody started knocking on the front door. Bam! Bam! Real serious knocking, like somebody who meant it so much they didn't stop to notice there was a doorbell.

Cath was focused hard on her screen, so she said, "Marmalade, go see who that is, okay?"

By the way "Marmalade" isn't Marmy's real name. I'm the one who started that, when we were in the third grade, when somebody said "Marmy" must be short for something, and I said "Marmalade." It just popped into my head like those things do. Somehow it got entered in the school computer—"Marmalade Albright"—and you know how it is once things get entered in the school computer. That year we had people in our class with names like November and Willow and Destiny, so I guess Marmalade didn't sound all that odd.

Odd is precisely how Marmy looked right now, coming back into the den after going to the door.

"David! Somebody wants to see you!"

"Who? Me? Here? Why? Who?"

"What language is *that?*" Dillon asked. Meanwhile I began to notice that Marmy looked like she was about to faint. Then she talked, and then I thought *I* would faint.

"It's Ripper Wilter!" she hissed. "He's *here.* I told him I'd check and see if you were around. I thought maybe you could jump out the window or something."

Well I didn't like the idea of being chicken, and anyway I knew I wouldn't fit. We were in the den at the back of the house, where you're almost in the woods, and through the window you can see the path going out through the woods to a spectacle-popping view of the lake. It's a paradise, except that Cathy's parents forgot to put a back door in the den leading out to paradise. In other words, we were trapped.

"Relax, David," Dillon said. He didn't *sound* relaxed. "What have you got to worry about? His trophy's back in his garage, right?"

"Yeah. Sure. Right! Brownie took it back. Didn't you?"

Brownie was sitting with his feet up, swallowing soda from a can. "I told you I would, didn't I?"

"Sure. Okay. So what does Ripper want, Marmy?"

She took a deep breath. This was going to be more than a four-second sound bite. "He said you've still got his trophy and he's going to call the principal and hold your face to the phone and force you to confess you're a thief and you're going to get kicked out of school!"

"What a joke!" said Brownie. He took a big glug of soda.

As usual, Marmy wasn't through. "And he said if Brownie doesn't get his Twins cap back to him by tomorrow at three o'clock p.m., he'll personally stuff it down his throat!"

Brownie choked, gasped, gagged, and snorted all at the same time. Half his soda was coming out his mouth and the rest was coming out his nose.

Cathy, rolling the trackball and squinting at the screen, made a request. "Will you guys be quiet? I've never made it to this level before and I'm trying to concentrate."

So there was a big heavy silence. I kept glancing at Brownie, and a little doubt formed . . . no, it *towered* in my mind. Was it possible that this lifetime friend of mine, this old pal, this original Jackpine Pointer, was a double-crosser?

And if he was—why?

Bang! Ripper was still beating on the front door.

Marmy and Dillon and I were frozen in place, and Brownie was blowing his nose, so Cath got up to answer the door. I looked around and saw the cordless phone sitting on the coffee table.

"Hide that phone!" I ordered. "We can't let him call the principal! Say Sugar ate it! Say Cathy can't afford a phone!"

Marmy grabbed the phone. The pounding on the door got louder. She ran off down the hall toward the kitchen, and I collapsed into the swivel chair at Cath's computer and tried to pretend I was focused on this game.

Why can't all of life's battles be won with the click of a mouse or the spin of a trackball? I wondered.

Heavy footsteps thudded behind me.

"Malloy?"

What a laugh! This was all a joke! I knew that voice. It was Brownie doing his Ripper act again!

31

"You got a problem, Ripper- Flipper?" I asked, still staring at the screen. "Just a minute, I'll be right with you as soon as I get to the next level and the next and the next. It'll only take me a couple of years."

A hand crash-landed on my shoulder and spun the chair around with me in it. The chair stopped and the room kept whizzing past. When the room slowed down, I caught on to a very important fact.

This *wasn't* Brownie doing his imitation.

3

A Rude & Thirsty Guest Shows Up

The first thing I noticed, after I noticed that he wasn't Brownie, was how funny he looked without that Twins cap he wears all the time. I wondered what had happened to it until I remembered seeing it in Sugar's slobbery jaws.

The first words out of Ripper's slobbery jaws were: "Get me a drink of water, Knutson! *Fast!*"

It's a shock when somebody says "Get me a drink of water" when you expect him to say (a) "Give me my trophy back!" or (b) "I'm going to pound David Malloy into the ground!"

Ripper went on grumbling. Obviously not in a good mood today. "I rode my bike over here a hundred miles an hour. Your dumb Jackpine Point Road is all dust! Why don't they build roads out of concrete around here?"

Cathy was acting uppity. I didn't see how she could stay so calm. *"That's* why you came here, Ripper? For a drink of water?" Maybe she was offended because Ripper called her "NUTE-son," when everybody in Bell Harbor knows you say the "K."

"No, I came here to get *him*." Ripper stuck his face in my face, so there wasn't much doubt who he meant. I kind of wished Cath hadn't reminded him. He growled, "It's all over for you, Malloy. Do you want a pine coffin, or would you like oak? Or can I show you something in mahogany?"

That was pretty good. I almost laughed before I remembered I was going to get destroyed.

Dillon decided to help me out by being brave on my behalf. "You can't beat up David Malloy! You're not strong enough!"

Ripper started rubbing his oversized arm muscles which I had never noticed before and didn't enjoy noticing now. "I'm plenty strong enough," he bragged. "I was Little League batting champion two years ago."

"Oh really?" I said with polite interest.

"Yeah, and don't pretend you don't know about it, because you stole my trophy. I'm still trying to decide how many places to break your face. While I'm making up my mind, you're gonna call the principal and confess and get kicked out of school. Don't say you didn't do it, because you tried to grab something else out of my garage last night. I saw you sneaking down the alley."

"Oh yeah? It was dark. How do you know it was me?"

34

"Because you were wearing that ugly sweatshirt of yours that says BELL HARBOR ISN'T THE END OF THE WORLD, BUT IT'S RIGHT NEXT DOOR."

Ha! I opened my mouth to tell Ripper he hadn't seen me, he'd seen Brownie. Inside my head I saw Ripper turn away from me and turn on Brownie. Good! He'd get what he deserved for saying he'd returned that trophy last night when he hadn't.

He hadn't, had he?

Of course he hadn't.

But how did I *know?*

That all zipped through my brain in about a nanosecond. Right in the middle of the zip, I heard an awful hacking and rasping. Ripper, who still hadn't gotten his drink of water, was hit by a coughing attack. I could have knocked him right down on the floor, batting champion or not. I almost felt sorry for him.

You know how it says "If your enemy is hungry, feed him"? Well, I didn't think it said "If your enemy is thirsty, get him a drink of water." So I didn't do anything.

Cathy said, "The water is kitchenward" and pointed, and I watched Ripper disappear down the hall—the same hall where Marmy had taken the phone. I shot Marmy a look full of meaning, the meaning of which was, "Did you hide that phone, or did you put it on the kitchen table where anybody with eyes can see it?" The only meaning in *her* eyes was panic.

I started wondering what I'd do with the rest of my life after I got expelled from middle school.

Cath was already sitting at her computer again. Didn't she care what a weird and terrible situation this was? Ripper Wilter, right in her house. Right in her kitchen! Guzzling

35

water from her own sink! How could she ever touch that faucet again?

Brownie moaned, "Do you think I'd fit through that window?" He looked pathetic, fear in his eyes and soda all over his shirt. For a second I even felt sorry for him too. Then I remembered how he lied to me and got me into more trouble than ever. When Ripper came back, I'd tell him who he had really seen in that sweatshirt.

Maybe.

"What are you guys looking sick about?" Dillon asked. He glanced toward the kitchen and dropped his voice. "What we ought to be worrying about is getting my roller blades back. It's almost winter and I have to get in shape for hockey."

In my mind I was going over my Brownie-did-it speech.

"I know!" Dillon had that megawatt look in his eyes that means he's got a scheme for *me* to carry out. "If they're not in his garage, they're probably in his basement. I wonder if his basement has a loose window. If his garage has a bad door, his basement probably has a loose window. Right, Cath? You're the smart one."

Suddenly Ripper's voice boomed down the hall.

"Hey, Cathy! Your refrigerator's ringing!"

I looked desperately at Marmy and she was looking desperately at me, and we both looked desperately at Cathy, who didn't get the desperate message.

Ripper's voice arrived again, louder this time. "Cathy! You hear me? I said your refrigerator's ringing!"

Marmy was waving her arms and mouthing "What'll we do?" Dillon was making motions for everybody to stay calm. Brownie was gazing miserably out the window. Cathy was chewing her lip and squinting at her computer screen.

"NUTE-son! Your refrigerator!"

Cathy put her hands on her head and pulled up two fistfuls of hair like she planned to tear them out. "What *about* my refrigerator?"

"It's ringing!"

"Well, *answer* it!"

Ever notice how when you get really scared enough, you get really brave? I went flying down the hall, but I hit the brakes when I met Ripper coming up the same hall.

"It quit ringing," he said.

"Well of course," said Cathy. "Refrigerators don't ring. Doorbells ring. Church bells ring. Phones ring. But not refrigerators."

Ripper growled and got back down to business. He advanced toward me. I advanced backward away from him. He advanced some more and I ran into a lamp. There was a world-class crash. Cathy launched from her chair and said "Mr. Wilter, I must insist that you depart away from this place this minute!"

She was bluffing, of course. What could she do, pick him up and throw him out? And I wasn't going to volunteer to do it for her.

For an instant the world hung by a shoelace. With his eyes shut down halfway, Ripper looked around at us all. Then he came out with a horrible sound, kind of like a chain saw mixed with a collapsing stack of pie pans. Later Brownie insisted he was laughing, but I could never be sure.

"Sure," he said. "I'll let you all keep worrying for a while. But let me tell you, where I come from, we know how to get what we want. You'll have that trophy back to me by Saturday morning at nine, or I'm going to . . . do something to every one of you Pointers."

37

Funny how different people are curious about different things. Right away Marmy asked, "Really? What?" As for me, I had decided I'd rather not know.

Ripper smiled a sneaky smile. "You don't want to know what it is. It's something I've only thought about, I've never actually done to anybody before, but when I do, you'll be sorry you ever messed with me. Got that?"

Then he looked straight at Dillon McBride and said something really odd. He said "If you want me, some of you know where you can find me."

He said "Saturday. Nine," one more time, like we planned to forget, and then he was gone.

The five of us looked at each other trying to understand what had just happened. I realized that Cathy's words had rescued us. "You saved my life!" I kept saying. "You saved my life!" She had also saved Brownie's life, but I didn't mention that.

"I have to do my homework," she announced, which meant it was time for the rest of the Pointers to leave.

I thought first we ought to return her telephone to the real world. I said, "Marmalade, you'd better take Cath's phone out of the refrigerator."

Cathy blinked. "My *what* out of the *what?*"

It was easier to show her than tell her. I led the rest of the Pointers down the hall to the kitchen and with a big swing I swung open the refrigerator door. "See?"

Cath said, "All I see is a gallon of milk, some leftover meatloaf, some mustard and ketchup . . ."

"Look harder," I told her.

". . . some brown lettuce—somebody really ought to throw that out—some leftover macaroni and cheese, some root beer. . ."

"Don't you *see* it?"

". . . some hard-boiled eggs, some celery . . ."

I stuck my head in the refrigerator. I saw everything Cathy had mentioned so far plus some other stuff, but no phone.

Then Marmy spoke up. "Oh, yeah, I guess I should have told you." She stepped forward, shoved me out of the way, and opened the door to the freezer. "Do you suppose this is why it quit ringing?"

Well, I'd never tried freezing a telephone, but I would guess it doesn't do the phone much good. That was what Cathy was guessing too. She was punching buttons and pushing and pulling the antenna and giving her ear frostbite listening for a dial tone.

"Marmalade, what were you *doing?*" she squealed.

"Helping," said Marmy.

I decided to walk Brownie home, at least to the end of his lane. By now it was getting really dark. A cold north wind was coming in off the lake.

Cathy's house sits at the Y where Orchard Road meets the Point road. If you follow the Point road, it goes out past my house and Marmy's and finally Dillon's, closest to the end, out where the Bell Harbor lighthouse is.

Orchard Road climbs the hill in the other direction, and walking away from all those other places toward Brownie's orchard felt—what Miss Wainwright would call *symbolic*.

I could feel something coming, some kind of bad breaking of something important, more important than even an arm bone or a leg bone. And I didn't know which side of the break I'd be on.

I wanted to talk to Brownie, but I guess I was quiet most of the way, because how do you tell a good friend that you think he lied to you? We had almost reached his orchard when he interrupted my thoughts by saying, "Did you notice how calm Dillon was through all that? When Ripper was there? Like he was above it all, or something?"

Now that he mentioned it . . . "I guess so. Why?"

"Don't you think it means something? I don't want to say anything against Dillon, but it's like he has nothing to fear from Ripper."

We had reached the entrance to Brownie's lane. I stopped in the middle of the road, and he stopped too.

"Look," I said, "anybody who's mad at one Jackpine Pointer is mad at all of us. If one of us is in trouble, we're all in trouble. Right?" Even as I said it, it nagged my conscience how I'd enjoyed the thought of Ripper turning from me and turning on Brownie.

Then Brownie asked straight out, "Do you think Dillon and Ripper are in on this together?"

Ouch! He may as well have hit me in the stomach with a silver statue. I yelled, "Of course they aren't!"

"I mean do you think maybe his roller blades never got stolen and he put you up to that raid on Ripper's garage, and then the two of them planted that trophy in your garage as a joke?"

I wanted to ask him right then. I wanted to say "Brownie, did you take that trophy back or didn't you?" Instead I said, "Brownie, what happened to the hat?"

"Hat?"

"Ripper Wilter's Twins cap."

"Cap?"

"The one that fell off him when he was running away from your dog. The one your dog retrieved to you all slobbery. The one you said you'd put in the washing machine and give it back to him. What happened to it?"

Brownie had gotten very interested in the gravel around his left shoe. He was stirring it around and turning it over with his toe and staring at it.

"Brownie, are you listening to me? Where's Ripper's Twins cap?"

He looked up at me. He looked down at the road again. He looked away into his orchard. He looked at a gull flying low overhead and turned to watch it fly away toward the lake. Finally he looked at me again.

"Uh, David?"

"Yeah?"

"You know that Twins cap that Ripper Wilter wears all the time?"

He knew perfectly well I did, because that's all I'd been talking about for the last half hour, but I answered, "Yeah?"

"Well, you know how I was going to put it in the washing machine?"

"Yeah?"

"Well, I put it in the washing machine, and . . . I guess it was set on ultra hot or something, because . . . well, and then I put it in the dryer, I guess I shouldn't have put it in the dryer, because . . . well, you know that trophy of Ripper's with the silver statue on it?"

"Yeah?"

"Well, right now that cap would just about fit that trophy."

41

I pictured that. I felt light-headed.

"That is, if we stretched it a little."

"Well . . . well . . . get him another one, then! There are lots of Twins caps, there's only one Little League trophy with his name on it. And by the way"—I felt a burst of courage and thought I'd better use it up before it left me—"would you mind explaining why that trophy never made it back into Ripper's garage?"

It was getting dark fast and I couldn't see Brownie's face very clearly, but he sounded all tightened up when he answered, like his dog had grabbed his voice and was trying to fetch it somewhere. "Don't you remember what Ripper said before he left Cathy's? 'If you want me, some of you know where you can find me'?"

"So?"

"So he was looking right at Dillon when he said it."

"So?"

"So maybe if we want to know about that trophy, we'd better ask Mr. Dillon McBride."

He left me and walked fast down the lane into his orchard. Still walking, he called back over his shoulder, "Thanks for not telling him about the sweatshirt."

In the dark I saw something darker hopping down the lane to meet him. It was Sugar. She was only a dog and didn't know what she'd done when she fetched that cap, but a person is a person, right? It seems like if we steal a statue we ought to know what we're doing.

But I didn't believe it for a minute about Dillon.

At least, I didn't think I did.

The next morning things seemed more or less back to normal. On the bus all the Pointers were their typical selves, and nothing Dillon did or said seemed any more bizarre than usual. Obviously Brownie had jumped to a conclusion, the same as I did when I thought he lied to me.

I admit I was a little nervous when I went to my locker before my first class. It did cross my mind to wonder what I'd find. When the last number on my lock clicked, I took a step sideways and eased the door open. Then I peeked in.

I saw bubble gum wrappers, some colorful rocks, sports cards, a half-eaten sandwich, and Dillon's pocket Spanish dictionary which I really ought to return to him. Nothing out of the ordinary.

Maybe the jokes were all over. Maybe Miss Wainwright was right, hope jumps up new with every morning. I grabbed my math book, slammed the door, and would have breathed a sigh of relief except that I was run into by Cathy Knutson and got the wind knocked out of me.

"David! I've got an overdue library book and I have to take it back right now. Will you get my math book and bring it to class with you? Thanks!" And she vanished into the hall crowd.

I was almost late myself, but after the way Cathy rescued me the day before, I would have gone and gotten a bear out of hibernation for her. I trotted down to the other end of the hall where her locker was. All the Pointers know the combinations to each other's lockers because it makes life easier and besides, we've always trusted each other.

I spun the numbers and swung open the door.

43

I discovered myself eye-to-eye with a serious-looking little person who looked like he was about to slug me with a stick, even if he was about 1/20 my size. The fact that he was made out of hard shiny metal didn't make him look any friendlier.

It was Ripper's trophy.

4
Suspicion Slowly Swells

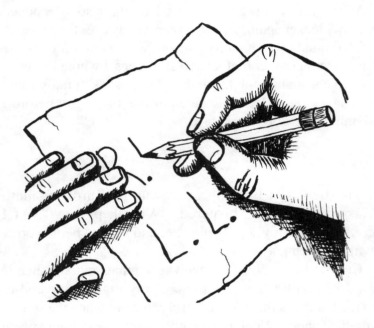

I slammed the door and pressed my forehead against the cold metal of the locker. To say my brain was whizzing in circles doesn't say enough. The truth is, I was dizzy. Everything got very quiet except for a waterfall roaring in my ears.

I re-opened the door a crack and dared a quick look inside. Maybe because of the shock of the past few days I was seeing things. Maybe the trophy wasn't really there. Unfortunately I wasn't, and it was.

I closed the door, more gently this time, and then I caught on why things were so quiet. The halls were empty and I was about to be late for math. Knowing our teacher, Mr. Grayson, he was bound to ask me why.

With great courage—at least I thought so—I opened Cathy's locker again, this time keeping my eyes tight closed. I felt around for her math book, but since I couldn't tell one book from another by feel and she keeps a whole library, I had to cheat and look through my eyelashes. Finally I laid my hands on it. I even sneered at the silver guy before I slammed the door in his face.

The bell was buzzing as I wobbled into our math classroom. Cath whispered, "What kept you?" but I collapsed into my seat behind her and handed her the book without saying a word.

Cath and I are both in the advanced math class, which is kind of funny when you think of my brain compared to hers, but that's the way our tests came out when we started middle school. None of the other Jackpine Pointers made it, so at that moment I had nobody but Cathy to tell about our latest disaster.

Mr. Grayson was busy sketching different kinds of triangles on the board. He gets very artistic about triangles and squares and oblongs and stop sign shapes, whatever those are called. I passed Cathy a note which I'd scribbled with shaking sweaty hands: "Have you looked in your locker yet today?"

She took a long time writing her return note. That gave me hope. She must be explaining why she had invited that awful object to reside in her locker.

Her note came back: "Of course I haven't. Otherwise I would have had my math book already. If I already had my math book, why would I ask you to go to my locker for me, because then I wouldn't need my math book. Why would I ask you to get it if I already had it? Otherwise I . . . ."

I wadded up the paper and scrawled another note: "Bad news."

She wrote back: "I don't want to know about it. What?"

I started to write a note explaining what. Then I imagined my note falling into the wrong hands. Too dangerous. I'd have to do this in code. But since I don't know any codes, I just wrote the initials "R. W. T." which any intelligent person should know means "Ripper Wilter's Trophy."

Cathy wrote back: "Runners Wear Tennies?"

I wrote back: "R. W. L. L. T." (*Obviously,* "Ripper Wilter's Little League Trophy.")

She wrote back: "Russian Women Love Lemon Tarts? How come every note you write gets damper and your handwriting gets worse?"

I gave up. Knutson may be an expert at computer games, but she sure lacks common sense. How anybody could fail to understand a simple thing like one of my notes was unbelievable.

Unless . . . she was faking it.

Unless she had that trophy in her locker because *she* stole it again *after* Brownie took it back. After all, she was in the alley that night too.

But what would she want with Ripper Wilter's Little League Trophy? She doesn't even like baseball.

Maybe she was going to plant it someplace. Like in Marmy's or Dillon's or Brownie's locker! But why?

47

I sat there trying to think what Miss Wainwright would do in this situation. But I couldn't imagine Miss Wainwright ever getting herself into this situation. Then I wondered if the Bible said anything about discovering stolen Little League batting trophies in school lockers. There was something about a silver cup showing up in somebody's sack, but it didn't quite seem like the same thing.

The effort of trying to figure it out had my ears ringing. And ringing and ringing . . . Why was everybody getting up and leaving the room? Cathy was standing up too. I didn't trust her; she was probably trying to get me into trouble for standing up in the middle of class.

"David, why are you sitting there daydreaming?" she demanded. "Can't you hear the bell? Didn't you get enough sleep last night . . ."

Her long list of questions was interrupted by Mr. Grayson's voice asking, "Miss Knutson and Mr. Malloy, could I see you a minute, please?"

I hoped he wanted to congratulate us on our great job on the last test, but I didn't really expect it. I was right. We stood in front of Mr. Grayson's desk, humble and silent. He said politely (but through his teeth), "May I see those notes you two were passing during class?"

I looked down at my clenched-up sweaty fist. If only I'd eaten them all. I handed mine over, Cathy produced hers, and we stood there motionless as silver statues while Mr. Grayson flattened out the wadded damp papers.

He studied the top one a minute. I saw his mouth moving. Then, very quietly, he said: "Roger Was Lost Last Thursday?"

He looked up at us.

"Racing With Large Lazy Tortoises?"

48

He was still looking our direction, but his eyes were far away. I mean they were still in his head, but they were looking someplace far off.

"Romanians Win Ladies' Luge Tourney?"

Cathy turned to me with her eyes bulging and I could see she'd gotten it *at last*. I yelled "Congratulations!" scaring Mr. Grayson half out of his chair and shaking him up so much that he let us go. The instant we got out in the hall, Cath hissed, "Dillon McBride did this!"

Well, that stopped me in my tracks, not that you can make tracks in a tile floor, because Brownie already suspected Dillon. Now Cathy suspected him too.

"Come on! Pick up your feet!" she ordered me. We ran to her locker, then we both stood staring at the gray metal door. She asked, "Are you sure it's in there?"

"I saw it myself. I ought to know what that thing looks like by now. I feel like it's practically one of my relatives. Here, I'll show you."

"No! Somebody will see the . . . you-know-what!" People were mobbing the hall, talking and laughing and arguing and crashing into us. I felt like a rock in a river getting smacked by every canoe that came by. Right then I would rather have *been* a rock in a river somewhere.

I heard Cathy groan. "I just remembered! I've got to open my locker! My ancient Egyptian history report is in there and it's due next hour!"

That was when I saw it all. I didn't like it, but the evidence was piling up against Dillon McBride.

See, after math class he and Marmy and Brownie always met us right here at Cathy's locker, then we all went to history together. It was a Pointer tradition. They'd be here any minute. And Cathy would be caught with the goods!

49

"It's a set-up!" I said. "Brownie was right! Dillon's in on this with Ripper—and now the two of them are out to get *you!* He'll stand here and stand here until you have to open your locker and then he'll say 'Aha!' Or actually he'll say 'Cathy Knutson! I never would have thought you were a thief!'" While I untied my tongue from saying that, Cath wailed, "What'll we do?"

She looked mummy-like, maybe because she'd gotten me thinking about Egypt. It was one of the few times I ever saw Cathy helpless. For once she couldn't double-click on the problem and delete it.

"Be cool," I advised her. "When the others get here, don't say anything. Just let Dillon know *you* know the statue's in your locker. And let him know *you* know and *I* know *he* put it in there."

"How am I going to tell him all that without saying anything?"

"You'll have to signal him some way. I know! Point!"

"Point? Everybody will ask me what I'm pointing at."

"Well . . . you don't have to point with your finger. Point with your foot. Here. Like this." I turned one foot at about an 87° angle to my other foot.

"What if Dillon doesn't look at my feet?"

"Jerk your head in the direction of your locker. And kind of wink." I gave her a demonstration. She tried it, and I was about to give her a *critique* as our English teacher would say, when I heard familiar voices that normally would have made me feel good. It was Dillon and Marmy and Brownie approaching and saying hi to me and Cath, as though everything was normal and fabulous, as though doom wasn't hanging over us like a swordfish, or maybe it's a sword.

"How was math?" Dillon asked. His attitude was phony

50

all right, I could tell. Like he meant more than he said and knew more than he let on.

"Math was fine," I replied in a voice that was rock-steady. "In fact we were asked to stay after class for a special talk with Mr. Grayson. Just me and Cathy. Right, Cath?"

I turned toward her and jumped in fright. She was standing with one foot aimed north and the other foot aimed kind of east-north-east, plus she was leaning towards the wall of lockers, like a pine tree that's been through too many storms.

"Well?" said Dillon.

"Well what?" I returned snappily.

"Well, are we going to history?"

Cathy had her elbow out now and her shoulder hunched and she was twitching her chin toward her locker.

"I suppose we're going to, yes," I told him in that same rock-like tone.

"When?" asked Brownie. "We're waiting for you."

"Yeah," Dillon echoed, "when? We're all standing here waiting for you."

"I suppose we'll go real soon, I suppose," I answered with a voice like a rock getting hit by a canoe.

Dillon looked at me, doubtfully. I looked sideways at Brownie, questioningly. He was looking sideways at Dillon, suspiciously. Marmy wasn't looking at anybody because she was busy looking for something in her backpack, which wasn't easy because it was still on her back.

"Well, let's go then," said Dillon.

"Right," I said.

By this time Cathy had herself lined up so most of her was all pointed in one direction, which looks fine if you're a Springer spaniel, but on her it looked pretty odd. Right then Marmy came up for air from the depths of her backpack and said, "Cathy, what in the world's wrong with you? You look like a Springer spaniel."

"Actually she *is* a Springer spaniel," Brownie explained. " They let them in on a special scholarship." I was trying to figure out if he meant to be mean or funny when Dillon announced, *"We're* going to class. See you later, after you shoot your goose or whatever it is you've got in that locker."

And the three of them left, and there went my whole theory about Dillon's set-up. Anyway the good news was that the hall was emptying again. It seemed safe enough for Cath to sneak open her locker and get her history report.

While she straightened herself out, I covered my eyes. "You do it," I said. "Please. I can't stand to see You-Know-What again."

It was dark behind my hand. I heard the combination lock turning. Three metallic spins. I heard the handle lifted. I heard the hinges squeal as the door swung open.

Then I heard Cathy, in a voice remarkably like a firecracker going off inside a cardboard box full of newspapers, saying "David Malloy, *you* are the biggest liar in the history of Bell Harbor. *You* are the largest fibber residing on Jackpine Point. *You* are the most worst bad joker in the history of bad joking. *You* are . . ."

I never found out what else I was. I stopped listening because my heart was doing jumping jacks for joy, like those sheep Miss Wainwright tells us about on Mt. Herman or wherever it is.

The trophy was not in Cathy's locker!

Then my heart fell with a cold wet plop like a rock dropped into the Big Lake.

If the thing wasn't in Cathy's locker, that meant it was probably somewhere else.

52

For example, in *my* locker.

I was trying to figure out how I could finish my career at Bell Harbor Middle School without ever going to my locker again, when I heard the metal door slam and Cathy's angry footsteps thud away down the hall. There I stood, all by myself, alone.

In history class I didn't know the answer to anything about anything. I got FDR mixed up with LBJ and the CIA mixed up with CNN. Mostly I was mixed up about us—the Jackpine Pointers.

All through class Cathy kept giving me disgusted looks. I knew she thought I was at best a practical joker and at worst a liar. Meanwhile Brownie kept catching my eye and jerking his head toward Dillon as if to say "Watch out for that guy." Dillon was Mr. Perfect all through class, shooting his hand up with the right answer to every question. Marmy kept looking at all of us in a foggy confused way.

At noon the cafeteria was cold and smelled like somebody had cooked the hamburgers a couple of days too long, and by the time I got to the food, the only cookies left were piles of crumbs. Dillon and Cathy and Brownie headed for a table where there were only three empty chairs. It seemed to happen by accident, but it felt funny that all five of us weren't going to sit together.

Marmy told them, "That's okay, I have to talk to David about adjectives." I knew she didn't know what she was talking about, because she called them "ad-JECT-tives." I figured she was upset by the tension in the air and wanted to ask me what was going on.

That's why it was no surprise when she leaned across her tray and said, "David, I don't really want to talk to you about ad-JECT-tives. The thing I want to talk to you about is . . . well, I guess I really shouldn't tell you this . . ."

"Then don't!" That's not what I said, that's what I should have said. That's what Miss Wainwright says to say when somebody says "I shouldn't tell you this." However, I didn't say it. I just let her talk.

When she talked, she said this: "I know something about somebody. Somebody we both know."

I didn't want to hear it. But on the other hand I did want to hear it, if you know what I mean.

"It's one of the Pointers," she said.

I figured that.

"It's . . ." Marmy glanced around and leaned further over her food. "It's . . ." I saw her mouth moving. I couldn't hear, so I leaned over my food. Then her eyes shifted to somewhere beyond my right ear and inflated about four times bigger than normal.

From behind and above me came a voice that was getting all too familiar lately.

"Malloy," said Ripper Wilter, "after you get done stuffing your face, you're going to meet me at your locker. I think you've got something that belongs to me."

5

Archaeologists in the Rain

Right then was the exact moment I figured it out: this "Feed your enemy" stuff doesn't necessarily mean food. I offered Ripper what was left of my hamburger, and it only made things worse. He thought I was being funny. As if I (or anybody in my place) could have a sense of humor.

So I kept eating. After all, he said he wanted to see me when I got done stuffing my face. If I kept stuffing my face for the next week or so, maybe he'd get bored and go away.

I took bites the size of pennies, then bites the size of nail heads, then bites the size that a fly would take. In fact there *was* a fly trying to take bites the same time I was.

After he growled at me several times—Ripper, I mean, not the fly—I finally waved him off—the fly, I mean, not Ripper—and finished my cold hamburger. I chewed it even more thoroughly than my parents are always telling me to chew. The time came when there was nothing left to do but swallow it. And then Ripper was curling his finger under my nose, meaning: "Come with me."

Have you heard there are times when you see your whole life pass before your eyes? Maybe that's why, as I walked two steps behind Ripper Wilter down the long echoing hall, I remembered watching a bear walk into our campsite and eat everything on our picnic table and then open our cooler and eat everything in our cooler. And I remembered playing Joseph in the Christmas pageant and forgetting my lines. And flunking an English test on Charles Dickens because I got mixed up and studied Emily Dickinson. And getting demoted to playing the donkey in the Christmas pageant and getting mixed up and reciting the lines for Joseph.

Amazing how you can remember all that stuff in the short time it takes to walk from the cafeteria to your locker, but I did. Then we were standing side by side in front of my locker, Ripper Wilter and me.

"This your locker?" he asked. He knew it was.

I squinted at the number. "Um . . . does that say ninety-nine?"

"No, of course not, it says ninety-eight."

"Oh—well, in that case I guess it must be mine. Unless they changed the numbers. They do that sometimes." I was noticing how deserted the hallway was. "Why don't you check with the office?"

"Why don't you open your locker?"

"I've got all the books I need, thanks anyway, Ripper."

"I said," he said, "open that locker, dummy."

Well of course that wasn't what he had said, but now wasn't the time to argue. I reached for my combination lock. I stopped in mid-reach. I frowned. I asked, "Now *what* was it you said you thought I had, that you thought was yours, that you told me you thought I had that was yours?"

I hoped I'd lost him, but unfortunately he'd stayed with me. "I didn't say."

"Oh. Hm. Then how will I know if I have it or not?"

"You've got it."

He wasn't leaving much room for talking this over, but I made one more try. "And you think it's in *there?* Huh-uh, sorry, there's nothing of yours in there. In fact there's nothing interesting in there at all. Just some half-eaten sandwiches and rocks and stuff. Definitely nothing of yours, Ripper."

He made a noise somewhere between a Canada goose going south and a tree falling into a swamp, shoved me out of the way, spun the lock, and jerked my locker door open.

Ripper looked into the darkness. So did I. I felt like that explorer guy when he discovered King Tut's tomb. I really expected to see a silver statue gleaming from the depths of my locker. But it wasn't there!

Ripper even had the nerve to stick his hands in among my stuff and stir everything around, muttering the whole time. Reports and notes and doodles skidded out onto the tile floor. I chased them. It gave me something else to do.

Ripper slammed my locker door, looked at me like I'd cheated him out of the Olympic gold medal in Bullying, and snarled, "You think you're smart, don't you? You're just lucky somebody lied to me. I'll get that trophy back if

I have to do you-know-what to you-know-who." And he stomped away.

I leaned against the wall, puffing like I'd just won the gold in the 1,000-meter dash. Wherever that trophy was, it wasn't in my locker. Of course, as I've mentioned before, that meant it was *somewhere*. I didn't like feeling good about me being okay when maybe the other Pointers weren't.

It wasn't till the middle of gym class, in the middle of doing my fortieth jumping jack, that I got the full hit of what had happened.

Somebody had given Ripper Wilter the combination to my locker.

Some traitor, I should say. That's the only way to describe a person who betrays secret information to the enemy.

I could barely manage my forty-first jumping jack. The only people who knew the combination to my locker were the other Jackpine Pointers. Then I remembered that Marmy had been about to reveal something important about one of the other Pointers.

Coincidences happen, but this was too much.

It was raining with a little snow mixed up in it when we got on the bus to go home. We all sat scattered, I mean none of us sat together. That was another first.

My stomach hurt. Just before we got on the bus, Marmy had handed me a note that said:

Come to my house. But don't get off the bus at
my house, get off the bus at your house, wait for
the bus to come back by your house, and walk to
my house. Eat this note.

58

I wasn't sure if my stomach hurt because I'd eaten the paper or because of what I was afraid she was going to tell me.

At my house I grabbed an apple and waited at the window while the bus went out to Dillon's at the end of the Point and then came back past my house again. Brownie was still on board—he's the last one off. I saw his face in the bus window and saw him look toward my house, and I backed away from my window.

I chewed my apple slowly. I didn't much want to go back out in the cold rain and sloppy snow, especially not to hear bad news. I mean, who needed it? I already had my old doubts about Brownie and now new doubts about Dillon.

I'd put it off as long as I could. Another ten minutes and the phone would start ringing. I hunched up my shoulders, yanked my cap down tighter, and splashed along the wet gravel road to Marmalade's house.

On the way over, I decided we could beat the situation with humor. Sure! Marmy and I would help each other look on the bright side of this.

I practiced laughing in the cold rain. First "Ha-ha-*ha,*" and then "Ha-*ha*-ha-ha," and even "Ha-ha-ha-*har.*" None of it sounded very convincing.

I jumped. Out the side of one eye I'd seen a black shape running in the shadows of the jackpines. No, nothing there. Probably my bad conscience. I ducked my head and kept going. It didn't help my mood any when, the instant I arrived, Marmy demanded "What kept you?"

Putting a little edge on my voice, I answered, "Nice of you to offer me some hot chocolate after my long trip through the sleet and snow."

"Oh, what's your problem? It's only a little ways down and on the other side of the road."

I gave up getting sympathy from her, and anyway she knew that I knew where the hot chocolate was. I got my usual mug and lit the gas stove to heat water. At our house we'd do it in the microwave, but the Albrights have a very old-fashioned gas stove. They like the old stuff. "More character," Marmy always says.

Right now she was saying "David, we've got a dilemma."

I shrugged and answered, "When life gives you dilemmas, make dilemmonade!"

"Is that supposed to be funny?"

Well, if you have to ask, it's wasted on you anyway. After we sat down at her kitchen table, Marmy began her speech. "I hate to have to be the one to tell you this," she said. She didn't sound like she hated it one bit. She stopped to look out the window and around at the walls and even under the table. "But I've found out that . . . one of the Pointers . . . is . . . not to be trusted!"

I took a gulp of my hot chocolate. "I know all about that."

I think she was astonished. I think she was even disappointed. "You do?"

"Yeah, and I think I know why. It's because this particular person doesn't have any . . . whatchamacallit."

"Any what?"

"Any whatsit."

"What are you talking about?"

"This person doesn't have any of that stuff Miss Wainwright talks about all the time. Industry? No. Integration? You know what I mean."

"No I don't, and don't drag Miss Wainwright's name into this. We've got a *problem* here."

"Integrity! That's it. That's what this person doesn't have any of. Integrity."

Marmy shook her finger at me over my hot chocolate mug and said, "She's a traitor, that's what she is!"

I jumped up, hitting the edge of the table and nearly knocking over my hot chocolate. "Marmalade, you'd better take that back! I can't believe you'd say that about our own Sunday school teacher! You'd better apologize—"

Marmy was on her feet too, yelling "I'm not talking about any Sunday school teacher! I'm talking about *her!*"

"Her who?"

"The Jackpine Pointer we can't trust anymore, that's her who!"

I stood there kind of dizzy while her meaning sunk through my skull. Besides Marmy herself, the only other "her" among the Pointers was . . .

"Do I have to spell it out for you?" Marmy demanded. "Okay, it's spelled C-A-T-H-Y, comma, K-N-U . . ."

I covered my ears. "No way!" I yelled. My voice sounded funny inside my head along with all the crazy ideas people were putting into it. "You've got no right to accuse Cathy! Especially after you froze her telephone! Didn't you see how she stood up to Ripper last night?"

"Yeah, and why do you think Ripper was so willing to leave? You think he's scared of a little computer techie?" Marmy sat down again. She had a very all-too-satisfied expression on her face. She announced, "I've been doing some investigating."

"Oh, no! I know something about your investigating! Remember when you investigated the other teams' ice sculptures at the Winter Fun Frolic?" That's a long story and I'll tell it to you some time, but let's just say the FBI hasn't come around recruiting Marmy yet.

She was going warp speed ahead with her accusations.

61

"Cathy sneaked back to Ripper's garage that night, after Brownie took the trophy back, after you chickened out!"

I started to defend myself on that chickening-out charge, but there was no stopping her now.

"Cathy stole it back and she's holding it for ransom! Haven't you noticed she's been acting superior to the rest of us for a long time? So she thought up a plan to use Ripper to get the rest of us into trouble so she can dump us."

Marmy's face had the glow of discovery. Like she just found King Tut's tomb or something. My head had the throb of overload. What really scared me was, she was starting to make sense.

"And to get his trophy back"—she was really inspired now—"Ripper's got to steal some new mega-power computer for her or something."

I sat down again. It did sound reasonable. I managed to ask, "How do you know all this?"

She paused, leaned back and announced "I saw Cathy with Ripper's trophy."

"You were hallucinating!"

"Well, she was carrying something bulgy wrapped in her jacket and it was about so big and she was carrying it like she was trying to hide it. She looked exactly like. . ."

"A thief robbing King Tut's tomb," I suggested, and we were interrupted by a howl from outside in the cold rain. Kind of like "Hal—lo—o-o-o!" only longer and more pitiful. It came again, closer to the house and more desperate.

"Ghosts!" Marmy yelped. Guilt, I guess. But I recognized that voice. You always know your friends' distress calls. "That's no ghost, that's Brownie!"

We looked out the back door, and there stood a dejected soggy figure in an Army-green plastic rain poncho.

62

"Have you seen my dog?" Brownie asked. Even his voice was soggy. "When I got home I found out she's run off. I rode my bike down here and I saw her run through Cathy's yard, but then I lost her, but she was heading this way."

So Sugar was the black shape I'd seen in the jackpines! By the time Marmy and I hurried outside, Brownie was already shouting "There she is!"

She sure was. Right there in Marmy's side yard, where in summer there are flowers if we haven't trampled them playing badminton, Sugar was busy digging. She had her front paws in a hole and she was throwing mud backwards in a big spray.

"Never mind the dog," said Marmy, who didn't seem to care that her yard was getting excavated. "Brownie, we've got something important to tell you."

"The only thing important is getting my dog back home. Wait, I've got the leash wrapped around my bike handlebars. David, grab her collar, will you?"

Sugar had her whole head in that hole by now and the mud was still flying. I went over to her, dodging pebbles. She pulled her head out of the hole, smiled over her shoulder at me, and wagged her tail. I don't know if you've ever been on the west end of a black Lab when it wags its tail, but it's kind of like getting clubbed with a tree branch. None of this helped my outlook on life.

Then I noticed that Sugar had unearthed a white piece of china plate or something. I picked it up. "Look at this! This is kind of like archaeology like Miss Wainwright tells us about. I'll bet this has been buried for years. I'll bet this is from prehistoric times."

"I'll bet you're a brainless dodo," was Marmy's opinion. Brownie was back, shaking the leash in his hands.

63

"Sugar!" he called. "Come!"

But Sugar had her teeth in something half-buried, something she didn't want to let go of.

"Hold it," I said, glad for any distraction from our worries. "Let's see what else she digs up. Maybe she'll find buried treasure and we can buy Ripper Wilter a whole Little League club of his own."

Sugar was wagging all over, growling a little, enjoying her work. "We're wasting time," Marmy said. "That plate is from some doll set I had when I was a kid. Believe me, there's nothing in this yard worth digging up." And at that moment Sugar backed out of the hole with a muddy shape clamped in her jaws.

You know those horror movies where a perfectly innocent-looking face gets gradually transformed before your eyes from nice to not-so-nice to something too horrible to look at? Well, that's exactly what happened as the rain washed the mud off Sugar's discovery. It lost its lumpy shapeless look and took on definite sharp angles. Then one end of it began to look like wood. And the rest of it began, dimly and then with a sinister brightness, to shine.

We stood there in a little circle, the four of us, and the only one of us who was happy was the one with four legs. Brownie and I looked at Marmy.

"What," I asked with huge self-control, "is that thing doing in your yard?"

She was ready with her answer. "It's Cathy! I told you so! She planted it here! She's trying to frame me! She's trying to ruin us all!"

Sugar put down the trophy. There were teeth marks in it.

"There's only one thing to do!" Marmy screamed. "David, you'll have take it back to Ripper's garage!"

"Back? Again? Me? Why me? Why is it always me?"

"Because you're the oldest!"

That wasn't true. Of the five Pointers, I'm right in the middle. I reminded Marmy of that fact and was even prepared with birthdays.

"I mean the oldest of the three of us here."

Well, that was a new one. I shook my head and started to walk away toward home. "Forget it," I said, and behind me I heard both of them pleading, "Please! David! Please!"

My heart squished up a little. Maybe it was the influence of the mud. I turned around and saw my two friends standing at the other end of the yard looking wet and sad. I started to say something like "Well . . ." when I saw Marmy snatch up the trophy, lean back, and throw it hard in my direction.

"Catch!" she yelled.

I was thinking she had a surprisingly strong throw, and I was thinking how interesting the silvery statue looked arcing through the silvery rain, and by instinct I was reaching out my hands to catch it, when a giant black object knocked me flat and galloped over me and left me in the mud.

"Marmy, it's all your fault!" Brownie was yelling. "You yelled 'Catch!' and Sugar thought you yelled 'Fetch!' Now we'll never get it! Drop it, Sugar, drop it!"

I rolled onto my stomach just in time to see a black Lab and a green poncho disappear around the corner of the house, and the dog was definitely in the lead.

I've told you Sugar is a Labrador retriever, but I have to admit she's not a 100% star at retrieving. When she's away from home and she fetches something, she doesn't always take it back to the person who threw it. Instead, she takes it home to Brownie's. Even if it's five miles away.

Brownie jumped on his bike. I ran up to my house, got

my bike, and rode hard after him. The problem was that we had to take the Point road, which twists around, while Sugar was heading home cross-country.

Brownie, urged on by the fact that it was his dog, outrode me even more than his head start allowed. I saw him disappear over the top of the Orchard Road hill while I was still panting at the bottom. There was ice in the gravel by now, and my wheels slipped left and right and backwards. I gave up and pushed my bike up the last part of the hill.

I was pedaling again and feeling pretty sorry for myself when I saw something sticking out of the ditch. When I stopped to look, it was Brownie's bike. I figured he must have jumped off it and was chasing Sugar straight through the orchard. That would be her shortest route home.

I decided to follow. At least I'd be under the shelter of the trees. Shuddering a little at the memory of one too many cold wet ditches, I stashed my bike, pulled some weeds over it, stepped over a barbed-wire fence, and went in among the dripping apple trees.

Brownie's orchard doesn't look so great after the first week of October. The big apple-picking has already happened, and all that's left is some shriveled apples on the trees and windfalls on the ground. I picked up one of the bruised apples and was calculating how much of it might be eatable, when my foot hung up on something and I fell flat forward.

I thought I'd tripped over a root, except it didn't feel like a root. And when I looked around to see what I was lying over, it absolutely didn't look like a root.

It was a person.

6

The Thing Disappears . . . Again

More exactly, it was a person lying in the long yellow grass with his head against the trunk of an apple tree and his legs sticking out of a ripped Army-green plastic poncho. Still on my stomach, I managed to crawl around and get a look at his face.

It was Brownie all right, and he didn't look very good. In fact he looked unconscious. In fact he looked so unconscious, he might be . . .

"Brownie!" I grabbed him and started shaking him and saying his name over and over. "Brownie!"

He moved a little and groaned. "Huh?"

"Are you all right?"

"Huh?"

"Can you hear me okay?"

"Huh?"

"Speak to me!"

He opened his eyes, blinked twice, and said, "Why?"

Well, I was a little offended by that. Here I am trying to save his life and he can't even find a reason to speak to me. But I'm pretty good-natured, so I overlooked it.

"Speak to me! Are you okay? What happened to you?"

Brownie looked left and right and up and down like somebody on a little boat coming out from a fog on the Big Lake, left and right and up and down, down and right and up and left, I was getting seasick watching him.

"Where am I?" he asked.

"You're safe with me."

He moaned, shut his eyes and rolled his head back onto the trunk of the apple tree, like he'd rather stay in a coma than know he was with me. It's like Miss Wainwright says, some people don't want to hear the truth. So you have to think of *ways* to tell them so they'll listen. I thought I'd try that with Brownie.

"Listen," I said, shaking him till he moaned again, "you're in the perfect place, you couldn't ask to be in a better place."

He opened his eyes. "Heaven?"

"No, your own orchard."

I stood up and shook a branch to demonstrate. Rotten apples rained down and unfortunately a big one conked him on the head, but it would take more than that to put Bobby Brown back into dreamland now. "My orchard? Really?"

He sat up and looked around. Sure enough, I thought, it works. I made a mental memo to myself to tell Miss Wainwright this story next Sunday.

Brownie shook the water out of his hair, knocked the heel of his hand against the side of his head, and shook his skull again. "Where's my dog?" he asked, like he'd jarred the question loose from his brain.

"I don't know. I'm more interested in that *thing* she was carrying when last seen."

"I saw her," Brownie remembered. His brain was unfogging by the minute. "Yeah, she was running away across the orchard with the—*thing* in her mouth, so I left my bike in the ditch and ran after her. I guess I tripped or something and clobbered my head."

I looked around at about a thousand apple trees marching off in rows into the dark. Dark despair, that's what I felt. "You don't think she buried it somewhere in the orchard, do you?" I asked Brownie.

"Oh, no. Oh, don't even say that."

He wasn't in any shape to hear such depressing ideas, so I asked him, "Can you walk okay?"

"How do I know? I haven't tried."

I helped him up. I could feel him shivering. I guess I was shivering too. It had gotten really dark, but we aimed toward the lights of his mobile home, cutting diagonally across the straight rows of apple trees.

Brownie's mom and dad were pretty upset when they saw the condition he was in. I was even more upset when I saw who was taking up most of the floor space in the kitchen. There lay Sugar on her stomach, all dried off and cozy, gnawing on a rawhide dog toy pinned beneath her front paws. She got up and greeted Brownie like he'd been away at camp for a week. That dog has no conscience.

"I guess she came home," Brownie said miserably. "She didn't . . . uh . . . happen to have anything in her mouth when she got here, did she?"

Brownie's parents weren't interested in what the dog had had in her mouth, but they were extremely interested in what had happened to Brownie. So he explained—with me helping, and him interrupting me and telling me he didn't need my help—all the events since Ripper stole Dillon's roller blades. I thought about mentioning how I'd found the *thing* in Cathy's locker that morning, but I knew it would only complicate everything.

After the two of us got our story out, Mrs. Brown still looked mystified. She asked, "But what was this trophy doing buried in Marmy Albright's yard?"

Brownie and I were equally much as mystified about that as she was. We both wanted to have a serious talk with Marmalade. Real soon.

Brownie's dad took us out to the road in one of the orchard trucks. The rain had almost quit, and in the headlights we found Brownie's bike sticking up out of the ditch, with mine next to it. We loaded them both in the back of the truck, because Mr. Brown had offered to drive me and my bike home without my even asking.

When I saw my house, my throat hurt. I mean it looked so warm and welcoming, the windows glowing through the pine branches. All the Jackpine Point houses look like that on fall evenings. It made me feel good knowing I had a home here on the Point, but I wondered if it would feel so good if my neighbors weren't my friends anymore.

Brownie helped me unload my bike and walked with me up my driveway. He didn't act like he wanted to leave, so we stood there, not quite facing each other, awkward, saying nothing. It was like starting up where we'd left off at the entrance to his lane the night before.

Finally he said, "I know what you're thinking."

I wasn't sure what I was thinking; I was only sure I felt confused. I waited for him to explain my thoughts to me.

"You're thinking I lied to you and I didn't take the trophy back to the garage that night."

"No, I . . . well . . . yeah, I guess maybe the thought had occurred to me."

"Well, I took it back. I told you in the alley I'd take it back, and I did."

Sometimes Miss Wainwright tells us, "You don't only have to decide *what* to believe, you have to decide *who* to believe." Standing there in my driveway in the fall chill, my hands on the wet cold handlebars of my bike, I had to decide whether to believe Brownie.

I thought back over the time I'd known him. (Since that was all my life, I had to do the instant-rewind, fast-forward version.) The evidence was that ever since I'd known him, he'd been a guy who did what he said he would do. Even when it wasn't the easiest or he lost something in the deal.

"Okay," I said. "I believe you."

Wow! It was such a relief to finally believe somebody that I didn't even notice when Brownie left. I heard the truck drive away, and I went inside my warm bright house.

Naturally my parents were curious about why I was soaked, muddy, freezing, and preoccupied, and why Marmy had been calling every three minutes and asking for me and then saying "Oh, it's nothing important." So I started way back when we tried to get Dillon's roller blades out of Ripper's garage and took them through the whole nightmare, which seemed like years but was only four days.

Of course they asked me where the trophy was now. As if anybody knew! I answered that I didn't know; I was scared to think about all the thousands of possibilities.

After I got into dry clothes and we were eating dinner, Dad told me I'd better call a meeting of all five of the Pointers to get everything out in the open. It was a good idea, as an idea—as something that stays in your head. In the real universe I didn't see how I could do it. Not when I didn't know who I could trust. Yesterday I had trusted Cathy and distrusted Brownie, and now it was flipped the other way around.

The phone rang again. Of course it was Marmalade, desperate. "David ! Did you find it?"

"No. It disappeared. Sugar probably buried it someplace."

"Then come to my house right now."

"Come to your house? Are you kidding? Last time I came to your house, I met up with that *object*. You come to my house if you want to talk."

"I can't. I'm grounded."

"Why?!"

"For letting a dog dig up our yard. Mom says I should have stopped her."

"Good! I agree."

"What? I can't spend my time baby-sitting dogs and tulip

72

beds. Anyway, listen. I called Cathy, and I think you'll be very interested in what she had to say."

Well, I was interested all right. I was also exhausted, cold, hungry—I'd barely gotten through my first plateful of food—and I still had homework to do. "Tell me later," I told her.

There was a two-second pause. "Okay, is this later enough?"

I stretched the wall phone cord as long as I could, reaching toward the table for my plate while trying to keep the receiver somewhere near my ear. I could hear Marmy's voice babbling on.

"Wait a minute!" I cut in. I had the cord stretched as far as I dared. "I'm trying to reach my food."

"Get on the cordless phone."

"I don't know where it is." I stretched the phone cord another two inches and myself another three. "Sugar probably buried that too."

"Ha, ha. Well, listen, here's what Cathy told me . . ."

The sound went dead as I fell into the middle of dinner, knocking the buttered rolls airborne into the green beans. I had pulled the cord out of the wall. Mom gave me one of her looks, but she and Dad are used to me by now, so I sat down again and resumed eating where I'd left off.

I decided to tell Miss Wainwright how God had stepped in and kept me from hearing gossip. It seemed like a long time until Sunday. I wondered how many places Ripper's trophy would show up in the meantime. Before I slept that night, I checked under my bed and in my closet, just to make sure. I also prayed that things would work out somehow, and soon.

In my dreams, little shiny guys with shiny sticks were chasing me on bicycles. I ran away on roller blades. I tried to hide in my locker, but I couldn't remember the combination. When I finally got the door open, a giant furry shape jumped out and galloped over me. Then I hit my head against an apple tree, and everything went dark.

Next day Dillon's Spanish dictionary scolded me every time I opened my locker door. Always before when I saw it, I would feel a little sorry I hadn't returned it to him yet, but I knew I could always do it.

Now every time I saw it, I pictured myself going up to him and giving it back, trying hard to act like things were normal. Like you do when things aren't normal at all, but you want them to be.

I still suspected Dillon of being up to something no good because of what I'd heard Ripper say to him, also because Brownie and Cathy didn't trust him now either. At the same time I wanted things to be back like they were before.

I practiced in my head. "Hey, Dillon, here's your Spanish dictionary. Sorry I kept it so long."

Too formal. "Say, Dillon, is this yours? I must have borrowed it a while back or something. Sorry."

Too casual. "You know, Dillon, I was cleaning out my locker the other day and I found your dictionary. I wonder how it got there?"

Too phony. I went back to Version A. I was going over it inside my mind, about to take the dictionary out of my locker, when I turned around and saw Dillon himself coming right at me up the hall.

I turned fast to face my locker. I snatched the book and stuffed it in my pocket. I closed the door. I headed for class—we were on our way to the same class, English—and I got through the door ahead of him and sat down. He sat down as usual to the left of me. Cannons to the left of me, cannons to the right of me, I remembered something about that. I sympathized.

I was trying hard to be normal. I didn't look at him funny or ask him any odd questions. I kept checking for the dictionary in my pocket, and it felt good to think I was finally going to return it to him.

Class ended. Dillon got up and I got up. He left, and I left, and I still had his dictionary. For the first time ever, we had gotten through a class together without saying a word to each other.

It was noon, but instead of heading for the cafeteria, Dillon walked toward the gym, and I felt a feeling I should follow him. The gym was full of echoes and people shooting baskets and people climbing up and down the bleachers. From where I watched from the lobby doorway, I saw him duck a low-flying basketball and start across the gym floor.

Carefully I stepped into the gym and peered around one end of the bleachers. It took me a few seconds to locate him. He was standing way over in the far corner. He was looking around, looking lost. I thought about crossing the gym and starting a conversation, when somebody appeared from a nearby outside door and joined him.

It was the last person I expected to see joining Dillon.
Ripper!

There they were, talking like they were old buddies! Well, not exactly. More like they were arguing. One of them would walk off like he was leaving forever, then he'd come back and they'd start their arguing again. Then they both nodded and walked away in opposite directions, Ripper out the door he came in, Dillon toward me.

I headed for the cafeteria, not that I felt like eating. It turned out to be pizza day so I changed my mind about not eating, but even the pizza turned to asphalt in my mouth.

Ripper and Dillon were partners in this together! Brownie was right, or maybe it was Cathy, I couldn't remember who said it first. And Cathy was also suspected by Marmy . . .

That reminded me. On the bus that morning Marmy had handed me a note folded about fifty times and all taped up. I hadn't found the courage to look at it yet, but now was as bad a time as ever. After I got it all untaped, it said:

> "C" claims she didn't bury "IT" in yard.
> Has ~~alabi aluhbi aliby~~ excuse. Says she
> was in school all day yesterday. Produced
> names of witnesses. Should we trust?
> Witnesses are:
> > "D"
> > "B"
> > Me
> > Yourself.
> > > — "M"

Well if I couldn't trust myself and Marmy couldn't trust herself, we all might as well give up. "C" spoke the truth, I had seen her in school all day yesterday. She couldn't have left and walked several miles out to Jackpine Point to Marmy's house and buried the statue and walked back to school in time to ride the bus home.

But what Marmy didn't know, because I hadn't told her yet, was that Cathy had had the trophy, sort of, that morning. At least, it was in her locker. I knew it was. I had seen it. Don't try to tell me I was seeing things. Well, I did see things, I saw the trophy, but it was really there.

"It was?"

Dillon's voice! Was I hearing things too?

"Malloy, you're talking to yourself! What's the matter with you?"

Dillon McBride was standing there holding his food tray, actually speaking to me like normal.

"You're acting weird lately, Malloy, you know that?"

Yep, he was normal. I felt relief. Then I felt distrust. Then I felt his Spanish dictionary in my pocket. Better hold onto it for now. I might need it for ransom. Or maybe it's blackmail—I get those mixed up.

Obviously the best approach to use on Dillon was the casual approach. "Talked to Richard Wilter lately?" I casually asked.

"Ripper? Why would I talk to Ripper?"

"Oh, you know," I said casually, "maybe your paths might have crossed and you might maybe have talked to him."

"Would Ulysses S. Grant talk to Robert E. Lee? Would Patton talk to Hitler? Would Washington talk to King George?"

Dillon plunked himself down across the table from me and leaned at me over his pizza. He was getting tomato sauce on his shirt.

77

"Let me tell you something," he said in that confidential tone all my friends were using lately, "there's one person you'd better not talk to if you care about your safety. That person is at the bottom of this whole"—he dropped his voice to somewhere between a bear growl and a rumble of distant thunder—"this whole trophy business. I know. I've got the conclusive proof."

He looked around the room like a spy who suspects he's being spied on by another spy. Then he looked at me with his eyes narrowed down so tight, I wondered how he could see me. Maybe he didn't want to.

"The person who is not to be trusted," said Dillon, "is Marmalade Albright."

7

For Some Reason I Do A Rescue

E at your pizza," I told Dillon. I meant it to sound
commanding and insulting, but it came out wimpy,
like a piece of friendly advice. More and more I
suspect I haven't got the leadership knack.

He leaned back in the gray metal chair. He looked very
proud of himself. "I bet you don't believe I've got proof,"
he bragged, "but I do."

Strange—right then I saw in my head a spray of mud and
rocks flying through the rain.

Dillon went on, "Marmy's the one behind all this missing-trophy stuff."

In my head I was looking into a muddy hole where something shiny lay at the bottom.

I told him, "McBride, will you leave me alone and let me eat my pizza? And by the way, most of yours is on your shirt."

I saw rain dissolving a mess of mud until a shape appeared, then I saw the shape turning silver. I shivered.

"Cold?" Dillon asked, as if he cared, then he got back down to business. "As a matter of fact, Marmy herself is in possession of—*the goods*— right now. But here's the worst part. She's trying to frame our friend Cathy!"

I started to object, but he was still talking. "Marmy called Cath last night and accused her of stealing you-know-what to try and sell it somewhere and buy some new computer or something. Then she claimed Cathy planted it somewhere at somebody's house to frame somebody else or something. I don't know, Cath explained it to me. I couldn't keep it straight."

I wanted to answer. To stop myself I crammed my last hunk of pizza in among all my teeth. Better not to admit I knew anything. Especially I'd better not admit I was *there* when the you-know-what in question turned up in Marmy's flower garden. It would make me look like an accomplished . . . an accomplished . . .

"What is it when you're in on something illegal with somebody?" I asked Dillon. "An accomplished . . . what?"

"Huh? You mean an accomplice?"

"Oh, yeah, an accomplice. Thanks."

"Why do you ask?"

I choked a little on my pizza. "Oh, no special reason."

"Compiling a dictionary?"

Dictionary. That reminded me, I still had Dillon's Spanish dictionary. I decided I'd better keep it a while longer.

Dillon was looking at me with that look on his face which was all too familiar. It meant he was cooking up one of his plans, which, if it was like all his other plans, would center around me doing something I didn't want to do.

"Here's what we've got to do," he began. I knew it. "Ripper's still got my roller blades, right? Marmalade's got his trophy, right? Okay, so you tell all the Pointers you're calling a meeting tonight at my house."

"Why would I call a meeting at your house? Why not at my house?"

"I'm getting to that. All right, so we're all there at my house, okay? Then you get this phone call that you have to go home. So you leave, only you don't go home. You go to Marmy's house and you find the trophy. Then you call Ripper and tell him you're holding his trophy for ransom and if he wants it back, he has to return Dillon McBride's— that's me—Dillon McBride's roller blades. We've got to show Ripper he can't just take anything of anybody's he wants. This time it's my roller blades, next time it'll be— I don't know, something. Okay, so you arrange to meet him at . . . well, it's your problem where and when you meet him, but anyway—"

I'd been trying to break in and point out to Dillon the flaw in his plan, which was that Marmy didn't have the trophy at all. Then I thought: How am I supposed to know who has the trophy and who doesn't? So I sat there playing ignorant.

Let me tell you, it was no fun not being 100% honest with Dillon. I wasn't used to hiding things from him or from any of the Pointers. It felt like we were becoming the opposite of friends. And the opposite of friends, of course, is . . . those people Miss Wainwright says the Bible says we're supposed to feed.

By this time I was sure that *didn't* mean I should offer Dillon the rest of my pizza. It wasn't that simple, and anyway I had eaten it already.

I looked around the cafeteria with some hope of finding help and sympathy. I caught sight of Cathy two tables away. She was looking at me funny. I knew I'd hear from her next.

Sure enough, after the bell went and we were on our way to our next class, she ambushed me in the hall and demanded, "What were you doing consuming pizza with Dillon McBride?"

I wanted to explain that he had sat down with me. I wanted to explain a lot of things. Instead I asked, "What were you doing calling him on the phone and telling him all that stuff Marmy told you?"

"How do you know I told him anything Marmy told me?"

"How else? He told me."

"He's got no business repeating private conversations. By the way, how did that . . . you-know-what-I-mean . . . wind up buried in your back yard?"

"My back yard?! It wasn't in my back yard, it was in . . . Who told you it was in my back yard?"

"Well, it was in somebody's back yard. You know how Marmalade talks. I couldn't figure out what she was babbling about. Say, have you got a knife?"

She was starting to worry me.

"I've got to open this." She held up a battered envelope addressed only to "C." It looked like it had something in it folded about 75 times.

"Oh, she's writing you notes now too, huh?" I said while Cath slit the envelope open with my pocketknife, smoothly and efficiently, like an executive behind a desk.

"Go elsewhere, will you?" she commanded. "This is a personal-to-personal communication."

"Hold on. First explain to me why you're talking to Dillon when you think he's Suspect Number One and he put the statue in your locker."

"I'm not positive the statue was ever in my locker. *You* said the statue was in my locker. You also wrote me damp unreadable notes in ridiculous code and got us in trouble with Mr. Grayson. And to think a couple of days ago I rescued you from Ripper."

"Yeah, I need to talk to you about that. Is there any possibility that Ripper . . . I mean, not that he has any reason . . . but could it be possible that you've got something in your possession that he possibly . . ."

Cathy had gotten all 75 of the folds in her note unfolded and was trying to read it.

I sputtered out the big question: "Do you know what ransom is?" She took time out from her reading to look at me like I had swooped in on the latest asteroid, then she went back to her reading.

"Or do I mean blackmail? I get those mixed up."

Cathy waved the paper at my nose. "Look at this! I wish some people would get a computer and write their notes so a person can read them!"

I was trying to read the note, but she was swinging it through the air so fast, the breeze was in danger of making me sneeze. "What's it say?"

"It's a list of accusations! And suspicions! And persecutions! Listen to this! No, don't listen to this. It's personal." She turned her back on me.

"Okay, okay, but give me back my letter-opener."

I had pocketed my jackknife and was walking away when somebody grabbed me from behind and pulled me against the lockers: BOING! This was too much for one day. As I twisted myself loose, I heard somebody besides myself bouncing off the lockers: BOING!!!

I faced my attacker. It was only Brownie. He whined, "Go easy on me, will you? I've still got a headache from running into that apple tree."

"What's the idea of ambushing me?"

"I was trying to get your attention."

"I thought you were Ripper."

I expected the name would make Brownie shudder or at least gulp. Instead, he grinned and whispered, "I found it!"

"You mean . . . you found *it?*"

"This morning. Out behind Sugar's doghouse. It doesn't look the greatest, but it's still in one piece."

"That's the best news I've heard all week! You wouldn't believe the stuff I've been through today!"

"Yeah, well, I sympathize and all that." He rubbed the back of his head.

"You've really got it? Do you know what that means? It means we can finally see the light at the end of the cave!"

The bell went again; Brownie and I had classes in opposite directions, and now we were both late, but in my new joy and happiness I didn't care.

As I started for my class I asked him quickly, "So when are you taking it back?"

"I'm not," he said. "I can't. I don't have it anymore." And he took off down the hall like a rabbit who's discovered he's made a blind date with a coyote.

Forgive me if my memory of my next class is fuzzy. I was distracted, not only by the latest Fast-Breaking Statue News of the Hour, but also by the fact that Ripper Wilter himself was in this particular class with me. It was a science lab and I'd always suspected he was going to blow me up someday. At this point, getting blown up was a minor worry. All I could worry about was where that statue was going to show up next.

After the lab, where my experiment of course fizzled, Ripper stuck close—too close—to me as I stumbled down the hall toward my locker. Not good. The way my life was going, Brownie had probably decided my locker was the perfect place to stash that trophy.

Maybe I could skip going to my locker today, and the next day and the next day and the next . . .

Up ahead of us I spotted Marmy, bobbing along like she didn't have a care in the cosmos, and I was jealous. She was probably thinking up new accusatory notes to write. Her backpack was a little loose on her so it bounced as she walked. It was always like that. She's never figured out how to tighten the straps.

85

We were coming up behind her, and I was expecting her to whirl around and accuse me of belonging to some major international crime ring.

That's when I saw it. Sticking out of her backpack where the zipper wasn't all the way closed.

Only a little glimpse—only a flash—but enough to be sure. A silver head with the silver bill of a silver cap. It would disappear down inside every few steps as she joggled along. Then it would pop up again like a drowning man coming up to look at the scenery and breathe.

I almost called out to warn her, but Ripper was right behind and to the left of me.

I turned halfway around. "Say, Ripper," I said.

It was the first time I had on purpose started a conversation with him, and I don't think he believed I was serious. He grumped and kept walking. I shuffled and skipped sideways to keep ahead of him.

"Hey, Ripper, have I ever showed you my pocketknife?" I fumbled through about six pockets before I found it and pulled it out.

"Funny-looking knife," he said.

I had pulled out Dillon's Spanish dictionary instead.

"Hasta la vista!" I said, doing a fair impersonation of a laugh. "Did you know I was studying Spanish? You should study Spanish. It might come in handy someday. You might play baseball in Mexico or something."

Ripper had his eyes front. I sneaked a look in the same direction. The thing was practically waving hello to us by now. I had to distract him.

No. Why should I distract him? Why protect Marmalade Albright, who accused her closest friends of treachery and blabbed people's secrets to the whole world night after night over the phone?

I stopped cold, thinking Ripper would stop with me, but he kept on going.

Fine. Why protect Marmy, who threw muddy statues at me and made me get run over by speeding dogs and forced me to ride my bike miles through freezing rain?

Did I owe her any favors? Of course not.

Had she earned any favors from me lately? Hardly.

I was thinking how undeserving she was and how I didn't owe her anything in the world except a cutting insult or two or three, when I shocked myself by discovering that my feet were moving. Both of them. They were running. I caught up with Ripper Wilter and tapped him on the back. His back felt solid and hard like a fighter's or a football player's.

"Say, uh, excuse me," I said.

He turned around glaring. "What do you want?"

What did I want? "Uh . . . I wondered, have you read any good books lately?"

I risked shooting a glance beyond his shoulder. Marmy's backpack was getting lost in the crowd. I took one long deep breath. Ripper looked at me like he thought I was crazy, which he did anyway, and turned away with a snort. But Marmy had gotten away. She was safe. And she didn't even know that I had saved her.

After school the bus was late showing up. It was a tense wait, because the other four Pointers were trying to avoid looking at each other or talking to each other. By clever navigation I managed to get myself behind the dumpster and motion to Brownie to come near.

"Marmy's got the trophy!" I gasped at him.

He looked very superior. "Not now, she doesn't. I just stashed it with her temporarily for safe-keeping because I saw Ripper hanging around my locker."

"Safe-keeping! She nearly dropped it in Ripper's lap!"

"I'm not surprised."

"She nearly handed it to him gift-wrapped!"

"I hear you've called a meeting at Dillon's tonight."

I blinked. I'd forgotten about that. Apparently good old Dillon had taken it on himself to call the meeting for me. "Okay, well then, I guess we've got a meeting at Dillon's. The more important thing is, have you taken care of . . . you know what?"

"Of course I have. Relax, David, will you? What's the meeting about?"

"I don't know."

"Huh?"

"I mean you'll find out. I mean . . ." Suddenly I recalled a quote from the famous Bobby Brown. "If you want to know what this meeting is about," I said in a voice of mystery, "you'd better ask Mr. Dillon McBride."

8
Phony Phone Calls

Through the jackpines the setting sun was shooting me in the eyes. I was walking as slowly as I could toward Dillon's house. All my life I'd been walking there, so often I could do it in total darkness backwards and blindfolded. You go out toward the end of the point, around a couple of curves, to where the Point road gets narrower and the trees start coming in on both sides of you.

Always before I'd gone out that way looking ahead to good times. Even when things were rough for Dillon or for me, we both knew we'd find a friend in each other.

This time everything was different. This time I was walking like somebody had dipped my shoes in rubber cement. My gaze was down in the gravel.

When I heard somebody walking behind me, I wasn't even curious. It was only to distract myself from my troubles that I bothered to take a look.

It was Cathy Knutson. Like me, she was on her way to Dillon's for this supposed meeting of the Pointers. But she wasn't hurrying to catch up with me. She wasn't even acting like she knew I was there. And only a few days ago we'd faced down Ripper Wilter together.

I turned my back on Cath and kept walking. I was coming up to the Albrights' house, and I saw Marmy come out her front door and start down the road ahead of me. She wasn't wearing her backpack. She glanced once my direction, then turned away; she didn't wave or wait for me or Cath. And earlier today I had saved her neck from Ripper.

We walked on like that, all strung out along the Point road, around the curves, through the thickening jackpines. When Marmy was almost to Dillon's, I heard bike tires behind me. Brownie passed us all in a spray of gravel, pedaling hard, and he got there first without saying hi to any of us.

His silence changed as soon as I got to the McBrides' front door. Brownie dumped his bike in the prickly shrubbery and jerked his head for me to come over. I stepped into the bushes with him, sticking myself with the pricklies.

Brownie's face was glowing. Maybe it was the porch light. He whispered, "I took care of it!"

My insides felt a few pounds lighter. Maybe everything was going to be okay after all. Like Miss Wainwright always tells us, the mercies of the Lord are new every morning. Of course this was evening, but the principle was the same.

I was impressed that Brownie had been so speedy. "You took it back to Ripper's already? That's fantastic!"

"No, I left it at your house just now. On your back porch. I figured you can take it back later."

"You did *what?*"

"Hey," he said with a casual shrug, "I did it for you once, I figure you can do it for me."

I swayed forth and back from shock. There was a gonging in my head. I caught on somebody had pressed the doorbell and that's what I heard gonging in the depths of the house. It sounded like the alarm bell for The End of the World.

The End of the World—I mean Dillon McBride—came to the door and explained that the rest of his family was gone for the evening. Something going at the elementary school. One by one we entered the familiar house. The place smelled like popcorn, but for the first time in my life it didn't tempt me, not even loaded with salt and flooded with butter.

My legs were numb, so I didn't have much resistance when Dillon pulled me into a potted palm and mumbled, "Remind me to tell you something later." I didn't want to know anything he was likely to tell me, but he let go and turned away from me fast.

If things had been normal, which they weren't, we'd have all charged down the hall in a pack on our way to Dillon's room. But tonight things weren't even slightly normal. We all very abnormally shuffled along in silence, single file, next to the wall.

It's very important here that I explain something about the McBrides' house, and later you'll see why. Their house is built into a hillside, so the front door where we came in actually turns out to be the second floor. Dillon has a younger brother and sister, and all three of their rooms are on that second floor. Dillon's room is in the middle. And there's an attic above their rooms.

Now here's the important part. Each of those three rooms has a trap door in the ceiling with a ladder going up to it, so they can climb up into the attic, which was designed as a play room for all of them to use.

Sounds really neat, huh? Of course that means all three of them have easy access to each other's rooms. It's one of those things that was great a few years ago, but Dillon thinks it's a big pain now.

Creeping toward Dillon's room, I shot to the ceiling without a ladder when somebody jabbed me in the shoulder.

It was Cathy. She signaled me to come with her to the end of the hall. I signaled her that I didn't want to go, and she grabbed me and pulled me anyway.

"I have to inform you of some vital information!" she said. "You know Dillon McBride?"

"I think I've met him, yeah. In fact, I think this is his house."

"I mean do you know what he did? He stole Ripper's trophy again and planted it in Marmy's backpack!"

"He . . . what? Now wait, Cath, maybe you're jumping to conclusions. Maybe . . ."

"I saw it today popping out of her backpack like a jack-in-the-box! Who else would do something like that? It's sabotage, that's what it is! Do you know the conclusion to which I've come to conclude?"

"No, and I don't really care. What?"

Dillon called to us from inside his room. "Hey, come on, the popcorn's getting cold! I don't know about you, but I can't stand cold popcorn."

"Don't trust him!" Cathy ordered. "He's the one who buried the statue in your yard! He's trying to frame you!"

"No it wasn't—no he didn't—" My tongue got tangled around my teeth. I fled to Dillon's room with Cath behind me, and we were all lining up to climb the ladder into the attic, when somebody grabbed my shirt and pulled me back out into the hall.

This time the puller was Marmy. "David!" she hissed, like she was afraid I'd forgotten my name. "I have to warn you! There's one of us you can't trust!"

"Yeah, I know, you told me, remember?"

"No! Forget what I said about Cathy! It's Brownie you shouldn't trust! Do you know what he did today? He had that trophy! He made me keep it for him! Then he took it back from me and he's still got it!"

That was only about 9% of the story, but I didn't know where to start, and Dillon was calling to us from the far attic regions beyond.

Marmy said, "Brownie buried it in my yard and then got his dog to dig it up so he could accuse me!"

"Has he accused you?"

"Not yet, but why do you think he called this meeting?"

"He didn't call this meeting. I called this meeting. I mean Dillon called this meeting. On my behalf."

She thought hard about that. Her face got an "Aha!" look. "Dillon *and Brownie* are in cahoots!" she decided. "Maybe Dillon and Brownie *and Cathy!*" She imagined she was still whispering, but her volume had gone up to near-full.

I tried to shut her off by saying, "Now hold on a minute!" but Dillon's voice interrupted me. "Come on, you guys! The ice in the Cokes is melting."

Feeling like somebody about to be an invited guest at his own execution, I climbed the ladder into the attic.

There's no furniture in the attic, just some pillows and games and things like that. We all settled ourselves on the floor like usual, except spaced unusually far apart. It looked weird. It felt weird. All of us facing each other and nobody looking at anybody. At the same time, everybody seemed to be looking straight at me.

Fine. Maybe it was finally time for me to take charge. Maybe here was my opportunity to set all this stuff right. Maybe it was up to me to get everything out in the open and on the table—or in this case the floor.

I still wasn't sure why it had to be *my* job, but I dived in. I said, "I suppose you're all wondering why we're having this meeting."

But I'd forgotten that Dillon still had his ransom scheme going to get his roller blades back. Politely but definitely he interrupted me, and giving an explanation about as clear as Einstein's about why he had to get more popcorn going, he went down the middle hatch into his room.

A minute later we heard a phone ringing. I knew what he'd done. He'd dialed his own number and made the phone ring. I used to do that and drive my parents crazy.

We listened to him answer the phone. His voice was far off, but he was making sure we could hear him in the attic.

"Hello?" he said. "Oh, *hello,* Mrs. Malloy! *Sure,* Mrs. Malloy! *Really,* Mrs. Malloy? I'll *tell* him, Mrs. Malloy!" A few seconds later his head popped up through the middle hole. "That," he announced, "was Mrs. Malloy."

Marmy screeched, "No kidding! I thought it was the Queen of England!"

"David has to go home," Dillon said.

Cathy hooted, "I thought it was the Last Empress of Russia!"

"Did you hear me, David? You have to go home."

Brownie howled, "I thought it was Cinderella!"

"Too bad David has to go home," Dillon said, pulling himself all the way into the attic.

I wasn't eager to go anywhere, but it would look funny if I stayed, because it's not like me to ignore my parents. I looked around at my friends, or were they my former friends? I wanted to blow the lid on everybody's accusations of everybody else. But I didn't know where to start, and besides, there was the little matter of that silver object on my back porch.

I wasn't feeling very hopeful as I picked up my jacket and started down the ladder into Dillon's room. I shot him a nasty look, but he ignored me. He was talking real nicely about how they could all stay and finish their popcorn. He was sure I was playing along with his plan and heading to Marmy's house.

I started for my house. However, I didn't go by way of the Point road. Instead I went down through Dillon's back yard to the bay.

On Jackpine Point, depending on which side of the road you live on, you either live on the lake side or the bay side. For instance if you walk straight out behind Cathy's or

Marmy's, you wind up on a black rock cliff facing the Big Lake. If you keep *on* walking, you fall a long way down into very cold water or onto piled-up ice, depending on what time of year you're falling. Cathy almost did that once when she was thinking about something else, but Marmy and I saved her. I mean, that's what friends are for.

Dillon and I live on the bay side. His back yard, the same as at my house, goes down to a small sand beach and a little boat dock. I stood there on his beach, hunched up in the chill, looking across the bay at Bell Harbor, where we went to school and hung out downtown and three of us went to church and where Ripper Wilter was thinking up new ways to get revenge on us and get his trophy back.

The bay was quiet, and the reflections of the lights were stretched out long on the water. I was trying to tell myself how peaceful everything was, when something nearby went KA-THUMP and I leaped upwards a couple of yards and a couple more yards backwards.

It was only the McBrides' fishing boat knocking against the dock. They'd have to get it out of the water soon; in a few weeks the bay would be frozen and you could walk to town on the ice. Out there on the ice was where we Pointers scored our greatest triumph—sort of—in the Winter Fun Frolic. Meanwhile, out at the end of the point, the Bell Harbor lighthouse blinked like it's done for a hundred years.

It was all the same as ever, yet it was all changed. Somehow that silver statue had wrecked the view across the bay. If I'd crossed the road, I think it would have even done the impossible: wrecked the view of the night sky over the Big Lake.

Or maybe the silver statue wasn't wrecking anything. Maybe it was what all of us were doing that was doing that.

Out loud I said "God, can't this all get worked out somehow?" Then I went home along the shore, along our neighbors' beaches, onto my own beach and up through my own back yard.

After all those times Ripper's trophy had ambushed me, after all its disappearances and re-appearances, I was actually surprised to find it sitting right where Brownie had told me it was. It was next to the covered-up barbecue grill, ready to knock into the bay any baseballs that happened to fly past.

I picked up the trophy. It was my first chance to really look at the thing without being scared Ripper would come along and catch me with it.

"CHAMPION," it still said on the wood base. "RICHARD WILTER." I guess it made sense that Ripper felt proud of it. It was kind of ugly, but I suppose if I'd won it and somebody stole it, I'd want it back too.

I thought about taking it back to Ripper's.

Then I thought about taking it down to the bay and seeing how big a splash it made.

Then I thought about seeing how much *bigger* splash it made dropped off a cliff into the Big Lake, where the waves might possibly carry it to Canada.

I had managed to fight off the temptation to give the trophy a watery death, and I was considering a new and even better temptation—setting fire to it in the barbecue grill—when the back door opened and my Dad appeared.

Dad looked like the greatest person in the world to me. I guess I don't always feel that way, but right then I did.

"Oh, *there* you are," he said. "Do you know something? That crazy Little League trophy of Richard Wilter's showed up here on the back porch."

"Yeah," I said, "I've got it. See?"

"How did it get here? Do you know?"

"Somebody put it here and expects me to take it back to Ripper. I mean Richard."

"Why don't all five of you take it back together? Maybe you could use this as a chance to make friends with Richard. I mean Ripper."

Well, the part about making friends with Ripper sounded like dreaming, but I liked the part about all five of us taking the trophy back. In fact, I liked that idea a lot.

"I'm going back to Dillon's with it now," I told my Dad. "Everybody's there. We'll make plans to take care of it."

"Just do the right thing," Dad said. I tell you, he sounds more like Miss Wainwright every day.

I had my strategy stuck firm in my mind now. With the statue under my jacket, I ran back down through the yard to our beach, ran along the shore back out to Dillon's, ran up the hill to his house, ran into the kitchen on the ground floor, ran up the stairs to the second floor where his room is, and collapsed gasping against the wall.

Dillon met me out in the hall. "Oh, it's you," he said, as if I didn't know who I was. "I thought we had burglars." He actually sounded disappointed that it was me instead of a burglary gang. He has no more conscience than Brownie's dog.

"What are you doing back here?" he asked.

I was too out of breath to answer.

"What's the matter with you? You look like you ran all the way here."

I nodded. "Yeah," I gasped. "Ran. All way."

"Did you call Ripper?"

I was catching my breath and feeling better. In fact, I was feeling really brave.

"No!" I said, daring whatever would happen to happen and I'd take the consequences. "No, I didn't call Ripper!"

"Good. Because it's all off. That stuff I said about holding the statue for ransom? Forget it. It's all off."

"But what (gasp) about your (gasp) roller blades? Don't you (gasp) still want to (gasp) get your roller blades back?"

Dillon didn't get it. "My roller blades?"

"Yeah. I thought you wanted to show Ripper he can't just take anything of anybody's he wants. (Gasp.) This time it's your roller blades, next time it'll be . . ."

"I found them."

"Huh?"

"Didn't I tell you? I found them today after school. That was what you were supposed to remind me to tell you later. They were under my bed."

I spent a moment letting this incredible new fact sink into my brain. "You mean Ripper *didn't* steal them?"

"I guess not," Dillon said with a shrug. Believe me, if I wasn't such a nice guy, that would have been the last shrug Dillon McBride ever shrugged. "Maybe Mom's right," he went on, "maybe I should clean under my bed more often."

"Then . . . then why did you send me out to Marmy's to get the statue?"

"I didn't. I sent you home. Your mother called."

"You mean that was a real call? All that 'Yes, Mrs. Malloy' stuff was for real?"

"Of course. She called to say they found the statue on your back porch. Hey, I just realized. You know what that means? That means Marmalade must have put it there to try to frame you! There's no limit to what some people will do, you know it?"

Dillon went back into his room and started up the ladder. I inhaled several cubic meters of oxygen and followed him into the attic, where I popped my head up into the saddest-looking crowd of popcorn-eating people I'd ever seen.

It was obvious, what this party needed was something to liven it up.

I pulled Ripper's trophy out from under my jacket.

"Here, everybody!" I yelled with my body half into the attic. *"Catch!"*

9

The Great Statue Battle

When the trophy flew through the air this time, there was no black Lab waiting and thinking I said "Fetch!" This time it shot straight to Dillon, who reached and snagged it. Instinct, I guess. If that attic had had an end zone, it would have been an easy touchdown.

"Congratulations!" I told him as I hauled myself the rest of the way up through the hole in the floor.

Marmy shrieked even louder than normal.

Cathy shouted, "What's *that??*"

Brownie yelled, "What are you *doing??*"

Dillon McBride only stared at the terrible thing he held in his hands.

Finally Dillon looked up and made a short speech. I can't say it was right up there with the Gettysburg Address, but considering the stressful circumstances, he did pretty well.

"This," he said, "is not mine."

He carried the trophy to Marmy and said, "Miss Albright, I believe you were the person who had this last" and handed the thing to her.

Marmy took it, I guess without thinking, not that she's a champion thinker anyhow. She got that look on her face like certain people get when you hand them a road-killed skunk. Then she screeched, "*I* didn't have it last, Brownie had it!" and threw it at Brownie, who was already on his feet when he caught it. His catch was flashier than Dillon's because he kicked over a bowl of popcorn at the same time.

"David!" he said in a voice buttered and salted with blame, "you were supposed to take this back!" and he lobbed the trophy at me hard and high. It ricocheted down off the ceiling, bounced up off the floor, and made a perfect upright landing in Cathy's lap.

She didn't appreciate it. In fact she made a short speech something along the lines of Dillon's.

"This," she said, "is not funny."

Cath picked up the silver guy by the bill of his cap, like you'd pick up a dead rat by the tail, if you were going to pick up a dead rat. Personally, I never do.

"Would someone be good enough to take this?" she asked.

There were no volunteers.

"In that case," she said, "I will present it to the person to whom I believe is responsible for bringing it here." And with amazing force for an underweight computer techie, she hurled it at Dillon while at the same time kicking over a glass of pop.

Dillon took the trophy hard in the stomach and made a noise that's challenging to explain. It was a lot like the noise you'd expect somebody to make when taking a batting trophy in the stomach.

Brownie looked at his watch, said, "Time for me to leave!" and started down the ladder into Dillon's room. Dillon hurled the trophy down the hatch after him. From below came a dull thump and then a bigger duller thump, probably the trophy hitting Brownie and Brownie hitting the floor, not necessarily in that order.

"Good! This is all Brownie's fault anyway," Marmy declared. "He stole the trophy in the first place and he's been trying to frame me ever since. Do you know what he had the nerve to do today? He—"

The other three of us were distracted by a guided missile launched up through the floor. It flew in an arc over my head and landed in a bowl of popcorn, which it neatly flipped upside down.

Surprise—Brownie's head popped up through the hole leading to Dillon's *brother's* room. He yelled, "Don't give that thing back to me! I'm through with that thing!" and his head vanished back down the hatch. Dillon yelled back, "You think so, huh!" and grabbed the trophy and disappeared down the third hole in the floor, in other words into his *sister's* room.

A small moment of silent suspense.

Then a big THUD and a lot of hollering as Dillon and Brownie met in the hall below.

From their conversation, we got the impression they were playing catch. One of them would say "Here, take it!" and the other would say "Oh no you don't—here!" They kept that up, back and forth, forth and back.

Marmy picked up a glass of pop that hadn't been knocked over yet. "The ice is melted," she complained.

"You could go out in the lake and get some more," Cathy suggested.

"It's not frozen yet," Marmy pointed out.

"I suppose you could stay out there until it freezes," Cathy replied.

There was plenty of ice in those two girls' voices to freeze *me,* so I escaped down the middle ladder into Dillon's room. I mean I tried to. Halfway down I met Brownie coming up. He shoved the trophy into my grasp.

Why is it we automatically take things people hand us? We'd avoid a lot of trouble if we didn't. But I did.

I wobbled on the ladder between heaven and earth, or at least between the attic and Dillon's room. Then I climbed up through the hole and begged, "Would somebody please take this?"

There was nobody there to take anything. The girls had disappeared, probably one down the hole into Dillon's sister's room and the other down the other hole into his brother's room.

There I was, in the attic, alone. Well, just me and the statue.

Suddenly Dillon showed up in the hatch to his brother's room. From now on to make it simple, I'll call them Holes A, B, and C.

"Where'd they go?" he asked.

"I don't know," I said, hiding the statue behind my back. "I just got here."

Dillon was coming at me. "You're up to something with

Brownie, aren't you?"

"Don't be ridiculous!" I was backing up, clutching the trophy harder, ready for action.

Dillon was still coming at me. "You've got a plot against me, don't you?"

"McBride, why would I waste my time with a plot against you?" I was still backing up.

He pointed and yelled, "Look out behind you!"

What a joke! Only a fool would fall for that one! I laughed scornfully and took a giant step backward. I stepped into nothing. I had backed into Hole A, or maybe it's C. One foot went down into space, the other foot followed, one hand grabbed for the edge of the hole, the other hand still clutched the trophy, and I dangled from one elbow which was hooked onto the attic floor while my feet fumbled for the ladder.

I heard Dillon say, "Let go of the trophy and grab the ladder!"

I let go of the trophy and grabbed the ladder. There was a sharp yelp from below. Cathy was beneath me and had gotten conked with the trophy.

"You threw it at me!" she wailed.

"I didn't! I fell down—I backed into—I fell through—well, I didn't design this house!"

Marmy showed up right behind Cathy. She had turned all gooey and sympathetic. "Cath, did he throw it at you? Didn't I tell you he was trying to get us? Do you know what he did? He made me get grounded by burying that thing in my yard and letting Brownie's dog dig it up. And then he . . . "

"I did *not!*" I said as Brownie showed up at the hall door and growled, "You keep my dog out of this!"

105

There we were, all lined up: Dillon above me, me on the ladder, Cathy and Marmy in the room, Brownie at the door, and the statue lying semi-conscious on the floor. All we needed now was Sugar, and somebody could have taken a group snapshot.

Cathy snatched up the trophy and flung it hard at Brownie. I could see the throwing wars coming, so I escaped back up the ladder.

My head popped up through, as I recall now, Hole A, and I was about to tell Dillon what I thought of him as well as what I thought of the design of his house, when Brownie's head popped up through Hole C, followed by his fist gripping Ripper's trophy.

"I told you to take it back, Malloy!" he called out like the attic was half a mile long. "So here!" And he threw the thing the length of the attic toward me, precisely as Marmy's head popped up between us in Hole B. She ducked and said "Hold on guys, you ought to be—" and I threw the trophy back at Brownie, and she ducked again and said "Now wait a minute guys, you've gotta—" and Brownie threw the trophy back at me and she ducked again.

We kept up the keep-away game till Brownie retired and dropped out of sight. I said "Marmy! Catch!" and she obeyed that bad old instinct and snatched the trophy in mid-arc.

I left her staring at the thing and dropped from the ladder and ran out into the hall, where I arrived barely in time for a head-on collision with Brownie. Shortly afterward came a series of crashes in Dillon's room. Marmy was tangled up with the bottom three rungs of the ladder, and the trophy was lying in a coma on the floor.

Cathy's voice rang out behind my left ear. "David! What was the big idea of putting that awful object in my locker?"

I spun around to face her. "I never put anything in anybody's locker!"

Marmy wailed, "Where did it go? David, where did it go?" I spun around to face her. "It's right there!"

Brownie demanded, "David! Did you hide that thing behind Sugar's doghouse?" I spun around to face him. "No!"

Dillon came down the ladder yelling, "David! Get that thing out of my room!" I spun around to face him. I spun too far and fell down. On my way to the floor, something zipped past my head. There were a couple of loud thuds—me and something else.

From my viewpoint on the floor I saw Marmy come out into the hall bragging "There! It's out of your room!" Dillon followed her out, grabbed the trophy and shoved it back into her hands. "I mean get it out of my life!"

Marmy sucked in a big breath and started to answer, but Brownie was waving his arms and hollering *"Quiet!"* He stood pointing at the thing Marmy held.

"The statue!" Brownie said in wide-eyed wonder. "Look at the statue!"

We all looked. Being still on the floor, I had to look up.

What Marmy clutched in her hands was distinctly shining, like it always had been. But now there was a difference. Now it wasn't shining like silver.

Marmy screamed, "It's gold!"

Cathy whispered in awe, "It's been turned to gold!"

Brownie said in louder awe, "The statue's been turned to gold!"

Dillon looked closer. "No," he said, "that's a bowling trophy I won in the fifth grade. Marmalade must have grabbed it out of my room by mistake."

Overcome by the stress of it all, Marmy dropped the

bowling trophy on the hall floor. It broke in two right in front of my face.

Cathy was the one who got straight to the issue at hand. "So if that's your bowling trophy, Dillon, where's the . . . the . . . *you* know?"

Dillon proclaimed, "I don't know, that's you people's problem!" and like a king or something he went back into his room and climbed the ladder. When I got myself back onto both feet and started up the ladder after him, his face appeared in Hole B.

"Malloy," he said, " if you think you're coming up here to my attic, you're mistaken. You're the one who got me into this. If you'd taken that trophy back that night like you were supposed to . . ."

Below me I heard Cathy say "I found it!" And with me clinging to the ladder, she rocketed the thing straight upward past me. I felt like the launch tower for the space shuttle.

Too bad. If I'd had time, I could have advised Dillon not to obey that urge to catch everything people throw at you. I could have explained how not catching things saves you a lot of trouble in life. But there wasn't time. He had already caught Ripper's trophy.

I dropped from the ladder, closed my eyes and covered my head. Then I heard Dillon's feet thumping away across the attic floor heading for Hole A. I opened my eyes and saw Brownie race past the hall door, followed by Cathy, followed by Marmy, followed by Dillon with the statue in his hand.

It was kind of fun. It was like a parade.

They all shot up through Hole C and I heard them racing across the attic and I heard lots of "Take it! Here!" and "No way! It's yours!" They all climbed or fell or tumbled down through Hole A and ran through the hall again single-file. They passed by like that a couple of times, and each time somebody different had the statue.

I went out into the hall and picked up Dillon's broken bowling trophy. I thought if I did him a favor and fixed it, maybe he'd like me better. He couldn't like me any worse.

I had barely gotten the bowling trophy stuck back together when the parade came by again. Cathy had Ripper's trophy and was doing her best to get rid of it. Just as she stopped and whirled and thrust Ripper's trophy at Dillon, I shoved the bowling trophy into his other hand.

The parade stopped dead. Dillon stood there holding not one but two statues. He looked like a person trying to wake up from a very bad nightmare and not succeeding. Then he looked at me.

"Malloy," he said, "this is all your fault! If Ripper pounds me into the ground, remember it was all your fault!"

At the same time Marmy started screaming, "He's going to get all of us! We're all of us doomed!"

And Cathy was insisting, "I had nothing to do with it! He can't prove a single thing on me!"

And Brownie was howling, "What if Ripper shows up now? What if he shows up right now?"

Through all that scramble and babble of words I heard my own voice. My voice was saying, "Our problem is not out there!" I was waving my arm generally towards the window at the end of the hall, towards the outdoors, meaning Ripper Wilter.

"Our problem is not out there," I repeated, "our problem is in here! *Us!*"

Wow, I had to lean against the wall for a second to let my own words soak into my brain. That had been really deep.

The whole house got absolutely quiet for several seconds. The only sound would have been the ticking of a clock if they hadn't been all digital. Then Dillon pitched his bowling trophy into his room and said "I'm taking care of this once and for all!" He took off down the stairs.

The rest of us stood stuck in place trying to figure what was going on. Then we got unstuck and followed the sound of Dillon's running footsteps through the kitchen and out the back door into the dark back yard.

Marmy was reciting, "Our problem's not us, it's in here. No, no, that's not it. Our problem's not in here, it's out there. No."

The shadowy shape of Dillon was running downhill to the bay. Marmy continued, "Our problem's not them, it's us. Is that what you said, David?"

Dillon's feet rang hollow-sounding on the dock; an arm went upwards; the arm swung powerfully forward as though he'd been the pitching champion of Little League. All quiet for a second. Then a ring of white showed on the dark water. From far offshore came the sound of a splash.

Cathy and Brownie and Marmy and I stood in a half-circle on the shore. Dillon came back from the end of his dock and stood facing us all.

He looked like a choir director, us being his choir. But instead of raising a stick, he brushed his hands together and made another short speech. This one was more in line with the Gettysburg one.

"That," he said, "takes care of that."

Well, at least one thing it did take care of. When we all rode to school the next day, Friday, we didn't have to wonder in whose possession that silver statue would turn up next.

We had all left Dillon's one by one the night before, not looking at each other, not saying anything. It was a miserable departing from the house. We all went our own separate ways home.

Friday morning it was already becoming routine. The five of us sat far apart from each other on the bus. We didn't say hi as each of us got on. We didn't walk into the building together after we got off. In fact Dillon avoided all of us by sprinting into school ahead of everybody else.

The future was a cold dark fog, colder and darker than the water off Dillon's dock. I didn't understand everything that had happened. All I knew was that the Pointers were through. We'd all still live on Jackpine Point, but we wouldn't be the Jackpine Pointers anymore.

I wondered how I'd ever explain to Miss Wainwright.

At least there was one thing I could feel good about. Ripper's trophy lay safe at the bottom of the Bell Harbor bay. I'd spent a whole week in terror that it would show up in my possession. Now, no matter what else happened, Ripper Wilter could never again accuse me of having his silver statue.

As I got ready for my first class, I was trying hard to feel light-hearted and worry-free. I attempted to whistle as I arrived at my locker and I yanked the door wide open with a careless yank.

Ouch! A book tumbled out and hit me on the foot. No surprise that this day was getting off to a bad start. As I bent over to pick it up, I focused my eyeballs on what lay across my left shoe.

Miss Wainwright always says that when we read the Bible, we should put ourselves back into the time and place of the people we read about. I'd never been very good at that. But from this moment on, I would have an advantage.

I now knew from personal experience how that guy felt when that stolen silver cup turned up in his sack.

10

The Longest Walk of My Short Life

He looked even worse than the last time I'd seen him. His silver shirt had ripped at the elbow, so the cheap stuff underneath was showing. He was swiveled on his stand like he planned on knocking the ball somewhere left of third base. His wood base showed the dents of several falls down ladders, not to mention the teeth marks of a Labrador retriever.

I covered him with my foot. He spied on me from around the end of my toes.

"Oh yeah?" he seemed to sneer. "So what are you gonna do about it?"

I picked the thing up, put it back in my locker, took it out of my locker, stuffed it partway into my pocket, pulled it out—it got stuck—put it in my backpack, pulled it out of my backpack, pulled everything else out of my backpack, and stashed the statue down in the backpack's darkest deepest bottom. Then I piled in everything I could get in on top of it. I even went to the library and checked out three books to top the whole thing off.

The only question left was—"What do I do now?"

Well, no, that wasn't the only question. There were other questions, for example:

"How did this thing get out of the bay?"

"Who put it in my locker?"

"Why me?"

and:

"How much of me will be left when Ripper gets through with me?"

I stumbled from class to class, learning zero and making a fool of myself every time I tried to say anything. All morning I saw the other Pointers sitting in their normal places, but I didn't talk to them, and I don't think they talked to each other.

That's why I was knocked over by what happened at noon.

I was sitting by myself in a more-or-less private corner of the cafeteria, shoveling in food, corn casserole or peas or something, I don't remember. I was thinking I'd better eat all I could to strengthen myself for whatever lay out there ahead of me.

That's when Dillon McBride sat down next to me. Next to *me*.

114

I had my backpack, with the trophy deep down inside it, sitting on my lap, which didn't make it easy to eat, but I felt an urgent need to guard it closely.

Dillon stuck a fork in whatever was on his tray. With the fork almost in his mouth he mumbled sideways toward me, "Guess you were surprised at what you found in your locker this morning."

I heard a clang. I had dropped my fork. I snatched up my spoon and kept eating. With my mouth full of whatever it was, I mumbled back, "What'd you do, swim out there and get it?"

"Of course not! That water's freezing!"

"Then how'd it get out of the bay?"

He looked away from me. Embarrassed. "It was never in the bay."

"Huh? You ran out to the end of the dock with it! We all heard the splash!"

He looked so ashamed, I almost felt sorry for him. Almost. "I threw the wrong trophy by mistake," he said. "It was Ripper's I ditched into my room, and my bowling trophy I ran down to the bay with." He sighed. "And I was really proud of that bowling trophy."

We observed a moment of silence in memory of Dillon's loss. Then he got on with his story. "When I came back in the house, I realized what had happened. There it was with its head sticking out from under my bed. Right next to my roller blades. Did I tell you I found my roller blades? Anyway, I knew right away what I had to do."

"What did you have to do?"

"I had to put it in your locker."

There was another clang. My spoon this time. Desperately I started eating with my knife, which didn't work. Between

115

chasing vegetables that fell off my knife onto the table, I tried to ask, "Why did you—what did you think you were— what was I supposed to do with—"

"Well I knew your locker would be a good place to put it for safe-keeping."

"Safe-keeping until when?"

"Until I figured out what to do with it. And you know what? As soon as I sneaked it into your locker, the answer came to me. I knew what to do."

"Yeah? What?"

"Well . . . I remembered you were the one who originally volunteered to take it back to Ripper's—"

My version of those events was a little different from his, but I was curious where he was headed, so I kept quiet and let him keep going.

"—so I figured you wouldn't mind . . . I mean . . . that you would be willing . . . I mean, I thought you'd be the ideal person. To take it back. Again."

Let me tell you something about me. I'm not much of a person for making schemes. All the same, in the next fifteen seconds I thought of about a dozen tricks to make sure I *wasn't* the one who got stuck with that job. I thought of lockers and mailboxes and backpacks and doghouses and even a garbage can.

Then I had a different sort of thought. Miss Wainwright says mercy always outscores judgment, and a soft answer prevents all kinds of bad stuff. Maybe if I finally returned Dillon's Spanish dictionary to him, he'd be so grateful he'd volunteer to take the trophy back home where it belonged.

"By the way, Dillon," I said, "not to change the subject, but I need to give you something that belongs to you."

"Oh, no, you're not giving me anything!" He scrunched

116

as far away in his chair as he could manage. Further, in fact. He fell off the other side.

I leaned down and located him through all the metal chair legs. "No, no, this is something else. Something I borrowed, and I'm really sorry I took so long getting it back to you. Here's your Spanish dictionary."

He climbed back into his chair and looked at the dictionary. "That's not mine," he said, "that's yours. I borrowed it from you last year. I just gave it back to you a couple of weeks ago, remember? I guess I kept it so long, you got to thinking it was mine."

I looked inside. In my own handwriting was written "David Malloy."

Dillon got back to the main subject. "So will you do it?"

If there was ever a time in my life that called for a snappy comeback, this was it. I stood up, picked up my tray, tried to get my backpack on, put down the tray, put my backpack on, and picked up my tray again. With tremendous calm I looked downward at Dillon.

"We'll see," I said snappily.

I spent the rest of that terrible day walking around with the trophy poking me in the back, reminding me it was there. My brain felt like it was in a blender. I thought of strategy after strategy to get rid of the statue and take care of Ripper Wilter once and for all and at the same time get back at Dillon and Brownie and Cathy and Marmy.

I mean, why not? They weren't even my friends anymore. Any of them. They'd all become my . . .

Enemies.

That sounded familiar. There was something about enemies, something I was supposed to remember. It was a quote, right?

117

Yeah. If your enemy is hungry, feed him.

I'm pretty smart, and I figured out that means if your *enemies* are hungry, feed *them.*

Yeah, but feed them what?

I started thinking of all kinds of food. Good food, junk food, people food, fish food, dog food. I thought of all the times I've seen Brownie feed his dog. He gives her bacon grease now and then, but he usually gives her that Hi-Proteen Healthy Dog stuff too. He tries to do what's good for her. Even when she runs off with trophies and hides them behind her doghouse.

And my parents feed me good food. Even when I pull the phone out of the wall and fall into the middle of the food they're feeding me.

Maybe the best way to feed my enemies wasn't through their mouths. Maybe it was to do something good for all of them at once.

Like something that ended this whole statue thing forever.

And so it came to pass—I think that's how they said it in the Christmas program where I played the donkey—that on Saturday morning I was once again headed for Ripper Wilter's house. But this time I wasn't sneaking up the alley. I was out in the bright sun with blue sky and clouds and all that, and I was walking up the street with yellow and gold trees all around. I was even holding his trophy out from under my clothes where the world could see it. And I had even called Dillon to tell him what I had decided to do.

With every step I was practicing what I was going to say.

"Here, Ripper," I was going to say. "Here's your Little League trophy. It showed up in my garage, so I guess I'm responsible. Not that I stole it, I don't mean that, I don't know who stole it, but anyway here it is."

Too many words. Maybe I should just say, "I found this, is it yours?" But how would I explain? Better to take the consequences. Get it over with and be done.

I was about two blocks from Ripper's when out the end of one eye I saw something move on the other side of the street I was walking down.

Marmy Albright! What was she doing in Ripper's neighborhood? I almost yelled her name, then I remembered we weren't friends anymore. She kept walking along the other side of the street, looking straight ahead, now and then sneaking looks over towards me. I knew that because I was now and then sneaking looks over towards her.

I came to the last intersection before Ripper's block. There was almost no traffic, but I automatically looked both ways. It used up some time.

Up the cross street was coming a familiar face. In fact it had a body attached to it, plus feet. Brownie!

He didn't wave, but the look his face had on was what I've heard people call sheepish. I haven't known many sheep first-hand, but he looked how they must look. Kind of embarrassed about being so dumb.

I crossed the street. Out the other end of my other eye I spotted someone else approaching from the other side.

Cathy Knutson? This was getting stranger every second! She looked at me, looked away, looked at me again, but didn't say anything. I was almost to Ripper's now, and I got to thinking that all we needed for that complete group portrait was Dillon—plus Brownie's dog.

119

Like a mirage, except he was real, from between two houses Dillon appeared. He was avoiding my eye but walking along solid and real as anything.

He joined the group that was collecting around me like my adoring fan club, except they weren't cheering or asking for my autograph. They were very quiet for a fan club or even for the Pointers. The five of us were walking together now, me more or less in the lead holding the statue, the others in an uneven squad around me.

I couldn't stand it. I stopped, and so did everybody else, and I looked around at all of them. My face must have showed them the question I couldn't say.

"We couldn't let you take it back alone," said Dillon.

The silence that followed was cut by a jingling collar, and Sugar bounded up and greeted Brownie, happy to be here as usual. I took a step and the others followed, and then we were at Ripper's house.

We stood there on the white cement front walk not knowing what to do next.

Clank! From around the side of the house came a metal sound like somebody throwing down tools. Then Ripper Wilter himself came around the house, dressed in greasy clothes, followed by a man dressed in greasy clothes who must have been his dad. It had to be his dad because he looked exactly like Ripper, only more so.

I think we were all surprised. It had never occurred to any of us that Ripper was a human being with parents.

He and his dad stood there looking at us. We stood there looking at them. We had arranged ourselves in a half-circle, with me the middle person and Sugar on one end, and I was holding the silver statue stiffly in front of me like I was about to present Ripper with an Oscar.

120

Ripper's dad drawled, "May I have the *ahn*-velope, please?" and then he went inside the house. I guess he figured that whatever this was, Ripper could handle it.

I managed to step forward and shove the statue at Ripper. He reached for it, but he was staring at my face and not at the statue. I let go too soon. He didn't grab in time. The trophy fell on the cement walk, and what I dreaded all along would happen happened. It broke.

The silver batter snapped off his wooden base. His bat came loose. So did parts of both his arms. His head bounced off his body. Much as I'd come to hate him, I had to admire him. Even lying there smashed on the sidewalk, he still looked like a champion.

Ripper stared down at the shattered trophy while we all held our breaths. Then, when our faces were turning purple, he said one word: *"Finally!"*

All five of us let our breaths escape out of our lungs. We sounded like a car when somebody punctures all four tires and the spare.

"It's about time that ugly thing got broken," Ripper said. "I never liked it anyway."

"But why—then why—why have you been—" Brownie was having trouble with words—"why did you keep—why did you tell us—"

"What Brownie is trying to ask you," Cathy interrupted, "is why were you after us all the time because you thought we stole it?"

"Which we didn't!" I said.

"None of us!" Marmy added.

"You think I don't know that?" Ripper looked at us like we'd called him stupid. "How do you think it wound up in Malloy's garage in the first place?"

Well that was something I'd been wondering for a long time. Ripper was staring down at the smashed statue and frowning like he was trying to get his thoughts lined up. When he looked up at us, he looked like a goat. I mean like a sheep. I mean sheepish.

"I had this idea . . . Didn't work, but I thought I'd try. I knew you guys were snooping around the garage that night—"

"Retrieving stolen property," Dillon corrected him.

"Which wasn't stolen," I corrected Dillon, and it was his turn to do a sheep imitation.

"Anyhow," Ripper went on, "I got this idea to take the trophy around—plant it here and there—say one of you guys took it—"

"What??" Marmy squealed. "You've been doing this? With your own trophy?"

"Yeah. I kept switching it around. You know? And putting it—like—where you'd think each other did it."

My first reaction was that Ripper Wilter had been one busy person. *"Why?"* I asked him because it seemed like he'd gone to a gigantic amount of trouble.

"Because . . . I don't know, you guys just get me. When I came to this school I found out that everybody else I can usually make do what I want. But you Pointers are— different. You stick together."

In my head I got this picture of Ripper going around pushing over crumbling brick walls, and suddenly he got to one he couldn't push over because it was all stuck firm together with glue or mortar. *That* was how he saw *us?*

"You mean you even buried it in my yard?" Marmy asked.

"Yeah. Skipped school that afternoon to do it. I was going to come out and say I saw Malloy plant it there and make him dig it up while I watched. I hear the famous dog there beat me to it."

Sugar was staring at the statue with her ears up, hoping somebody would throw it and say "Fetch!"

One detail still confused me. "But who gave you the combinations to our lockers?"

"Combinations? Oh, that was easy. I swiped those from— I mean I got those from the office not long after school started. Comes in handy for things like putting firecrackers in people's lockers. I mean, I think it would. I've never done it. Talking about it's usually enough. The other day I found out McBride here forgot his combination, and I offered to give it to him. For a price, but he wouldn't."

I looked at Dillon and asked, "That wouldn't have been during lunch hour in the gym, would it?"

Dillon studied his shoe toes. "I didn't feel like asking any of you guys," he admitted. "The way we were getting along right then. Or not getting along."

"It gets to me," Ripper went on. "How no matter what happens, you keep on being such good friends."

I looked around at the Jackpine Pointers. There was Dillon, who sent me to risk my neck carrying out his schemes and forgot to tell me he found his roller blades. And there was Marmy, who dragged me to her house in the rain to tell me how Cathy was guilty. And Cathy, who thought I was the world's worst practical joker and I couldn't even pass notes right. And Brownie, who left missing trophies on my back porch and expected me to dispose of them for him.

We were such good *friends?*

And here I'd thought we were always going to be enemies.

It was Marmy who started it. She giggled, most likely because she was embarrassed. Then Brownie started in

123

laughing, maybe at her, maybe at all of us. I couldn't help it, I started laughing too. Soon Dillon joined us, first a chuckle, then a cackle, then a side-aching roar. By then Cathy had gone from a hoot to a howl of laughter.

We couldn't stop. We laughed till we hurt. Brownie even fell down holding his stomach. Sugar danced around wagging her tail and yelping.

In the middle of it all I heard an odd noise, not quite like a cross between a chain saw and a stack of pie pans falling over, more like a blue jay and crow fighting over a bread crust. I looked to make sure.

I was right.

It was Ripper laughing.

So if you want to see that Little League trophy today, all glued back together again, it's in Miss Wainwright's classroom on top of the green file cabinet. Ripper donated it and even threw in his shrunken Twins cap which just about fits it perfectly. We've invited Ripper to come some Sunday and visit it. So far he's said no.

Miss Wainwright says the batting statue is symbolic. If I understand what she means, I think she's right. To me it stands for how every time the Jackpine Pointers get thrown a mean curve, we turn out to be champion friends. Or at least we keep trying.

It reminds me of the time we entered the Winter Fun Frolic to build the best ice sculpture on the bay. See, the prize was a snowmobile and we got trapped in a spy ring . . . but here comes Dillon, with that look in his eye, so I guess that's a story you'll just have to wait for.

Want a preview of

Ice Festival

the next Jackpine Point Adventure?

Turn the page!

L et's tell jokes to keep our minds off the cold," Dillon suggested. "I'll go first."

We were sitting on three feet of ice in the middle of the Bell Harbor bay. It was midnight and twenty degrees below zero. Twenty real degrees, not your wind chill stuff.

"I'll go first. Okay. There's these two polar bears, and they're walking down the street, see, and one of them says to the other—"

"Polar bears can't talk," Cathy's voice came from somewhere down deep inside her parka hood. Or deep inside her down parka hood.

"Well, let's say these *can*. Where was I? Oh, yeah. These two polar bears are walking down the street, and one of them says to the other—"

"Ha ha ha ha ha!"

I jumped a foot straight upward off the ice and found the air wasn't any warmer up there. Marmy was laughing hysterically, sending round puffs of icy breath floating over our heads.

Dillon protested, "It's not funny yet, I'm not finished," and at that instant a flashlight flooded us with light, but unfortunately not with warmth. On the far side of the light a rough voice demanded, "Who's there?"

"Nobody but us polar bears!" Brownie answered.

And then came the sound of breaking ice.

Grab your snow boots and come along

. . . on the next Jackpine Point Adventure!

Merritt Park Press
3912 W. 7th Street
Duluth MN 55807
dslarsen@spacestar.net
(218) 628-0618